THE COMPLETE TALES OF
MERRY GOLD

THE COMPLETE TALES OF
MERRY GOLD

KATE BERNHEIMER

FC2

TUSCALOOSA

The University of Alabama Press
Tuscaloosa, Alabama 35487-0380

Published by FC2, an imprint of the University of Alabama Press, with
support provided by Florida State University and the Publications Unit of
the Department of English at Illinois State University

Address all editorial inquiries to: Fiction Collective Two, Florida State
University, c/o English Department, Tallahassee, FL 32306-1580

☉

The paper on which this book is printed meets the minimum requirements
of American National Standard for Information Sciences—Permanence
of Paper for Printed Library Materials, ANSI Z39.48–1984

Library of Congress Cataloging-in-Publication Data
Bernheimer, Kate.
    The complete tales of Merry Gold / Kate Bernheimer.— 1st ed.
        p. cm.
    "Fiction Collective Two"
    ISBN-13: 978-1-57366-131-7 (pbk. : alk. paper)
    ISBN-10: 1-57366-131-7 (pbk. : alk. paper)
    1. Fairy tales—Adaptations. 2. Young women—Fiction. I. Title.
    PS3602.E76C663 2006
    813'.54—dc22
                                2006006892

Cover Design: Lou Robinson
Book Design: Holli Kober and Tara Reeser
Typeface: Caslon
Produced and printed in the United States of America

The author wishes to acknowledge the German, Russian, and Yiddish fairy tales of her cultural heritage, on which portions of this novel are based.

From the German:

"The Star Talers," "The Hazel Branch," "The Old Beggar-woman," "The Three Spinners," "The Crumbs on the Table," "The Stolen Pennies," "The Bright Sun Will Bring It to Light," "The Water Nixie," "Mary's Glass," "A Riddling Tale," "The Coal, the Straw, and the Bean"

from *Grimms' Tales for Young and Old: The Complete Stories*, translated by Ralph Manheim (Anchor Books)

From the Russian:

"The Lazy Maiden," "Know Not," "The Bladder, the Straw, and the Shoe," "The Two Rivers," "The Beggar's Plan," "The Goat Comes Back"

from *Russian Fairy Tales*, collected by Aleksandr Afanas'Ev, translated by Norbert Guterman (Pantheon Books)

From the Yiddish:

"The Shretele That Took a Little Nip," "The Naughty Little Girl," "The Princess and Vanke, the Shoemaker's Son"

from *Yiddish Folktales*, edited by Beatrice Silverman Weinreich and translated by Leonard Wolf (Pantheon Books)

The author also wishes to acknowledge the fairy tales re-produced by permission of the publishers in their complete translated form. They are listed in the order in which they appear in the novel.

"The Crumbs on the Table" © Anchor Books

"The Stolen Pennies" © Anchor Books

"Upon Me" © Pantheon Books

"The Louse and the Flea" © Pantheon Books

"The Bladder, the Straw, and the Shoe" © Pantheon Books

In the folktale—perhaps for the first time—the world finds poetic expression. What in the real world is difficult, complex, and characterized by obscure interactions becomes in the folktale light and transparent and adapts itself with effortless ease to the interplay of all things. Whereas in the real world we see only partial developments and well-nigh incomprehensible fates, the folktale presents us with a world of events that is blissfully self-sufficient, a world in which each element has its exactly designated place. Furthermore, in the folktale we cannot see "behind things"; we see only the acting characters, not their whence and whither, their why and wherefore...the interrelationships on which the total structure is based are illuminated just as little as in the real world; everything in the background remains in the dark. All that takes place in the illuminated foreground is so clearly depicted and so much in harmony with itself, however, that the portrayal fills one with blissful assurance. People who find themselves hurled into a threatening world whose meaning they do not know; people who in legends create the ghosts of this uncanny world out of their lyrical consternation—these people experience the transformation of this very same world in the quiet, epic vision of the folktale.

—Max Luthi

Folklore is filled with ditties inviting the snail to show its horns. Children love to tease it with a blade of grass to make it go back into its shell, and the most unexpected comparisons have been made to explain this retreat. According to one biologist, "a snail withdraws into its kiosk the way a girl who has been teased goes and cries in her room."

—Gaston Bachelard

chapter one

A Whirly-Gig Tale

L ong ago I reached the end of my luck. Yet when I was a child I lay in my cradle asleep. *"Ladybug, ladybug, fly away home, your house is on fire, your children alone"* I played in my mind. My mother came in and said, "So you've gone to dreaming, my pretty? *Gey schluffen.* In the meantime, go down to the kitchen and wash a handful of grapes. I'll be glad to have them when I wake up." Then she plucked me out of the cradle, climbed in it herself and screwed her eyes shut. I crept down to the kitchen to get the grapes. Now, don't cover your ears, but when I reached into the fridge a viper shot out and headed right for me. Leaving the green grapes untouched, I ran away very fast. (After that, my father came into the kitchen and popped grapes into his mouth, one after the other, one after the other again.) All the while, my mother slept in that crib, curled like a roly-poly into a ball. And as for me? The viper chased me and chased me, slithering fast on the ground. This went on for hours until I hid behind a maple tree, shaking mad. The viper crept slowly away. This is why, since my earliest days, I plant a whirly-gig right on my nose whenever I'm mad. It provides a very strong message to vipers and creatures that crawl close to the ground—inchworms and earthworms and seals. I've reached the end of my story and also the end of my luck. Would you hand me a glassful of vodka?

chapter two

"M̲on-kee-kee," Merry said dispassionately, star-ing at the brown stuffed monkey in denim jeans that bounced from the nursery ceiling. The monkey wore a pink plastic helmet on its head, which sprouted a long metal spring. The pink helmet was its distinctive feature, and it de-fined the monkey far more than its painted-on, wan little smile. From what would its helmet protect? Oh, very much! For everything in the Gold household was designed to pro-tect: Mrs Gold didn't even keep knives sharper than butter.

Merry Gold, *nee* Meredith, shared a bedroom with her little sister, the insufferable Ketzia-who-never-stopped-cry-ing. In fact Merry had devised a small game in order to deal with her sister's sniffling; it was organized around the simple notion that a crybaby must be made to cry as often as pos-sible. Ideas such as these slipped easily into Merry's head, perhaps because she shared this stuffy room with the weep-ing sister and because of the room's musty tangerine curtains and heavy-breathing humidifier, hissing all the time. Mr and Mrs Gold did not know about Merry's games. Down the long narrow hallway they slept. "My Mon-kee," Merry said, kicking a stuffed monkey's feet, hoping to smash it into the wall like that frog from the story. It just bounced again, sprung through the air willy-nilly.

Merry looked out the window at the dead-end street. The boy from next door, the one with the wooden leg, ran after a ball. Merry envied the boy, but was troubled by his mother, who sliced off the boy's pants at the knee on the leg made of wood. Why? Seeing him wobble down the street in asymmetrical pants, Merry had the distinct urge to run after him and push him to the ground. Not for the wooden leg—for the mother.

Merry gazed at his wooden leg—the pegginess of it pleased her. She often amputated the legs of dolls and wished very much that she too lacked a limb. She glanced over at Ketzia. Did a crybaby need both of her legs? Merry turned to look out the window again.

For the vision of a limping boy was far more pleasing than that of her sister. And the vision of outside was better than in. Almost anything was more pleasing than the biggest, the most patient face in the room: that of a giant seal toy with sharp plastic whiskers sticking out of its nose. It lumbered on iron wheels that groaned; it dominated the room with a hairy body and smell; and it frightened Merry with its kindly eyes.

The boy's mother called him inside; *tap-tap* went his leg, *tap-tap*, goodbye. Merry's naptime was ruined. She narrowed her eyes at the seal and then at her sister. They had no right to live here, no right here at all.

chapter three

THE STAR NICKELS

I'm going to tell you something, so listen. Long ago I reached the end of my luck. Then I began to drink vodka. I was so bad that I had no friends to rely on and no one but pigeons to talk to. I lived in a small room and slept on the floor, on what was known as the avenue of diamonds. You could hear the taxis and trucks through the windows and fights in the hall through the vents.

I'd long ago left my parents' house and all childhood trinkets behind—a rabbit fur coat, sugared eggs with little chickens inside, a machine that could polish rocks. I was too upset to ask for help. And my only friends in the world both had died.

I was awake a lot of the time. This was in a big city that was filled with trouble. They announced it on the television, and in the papers. I spent my nights walking the square under the bright lights in a leather jacket Semyon and Tibor had gotten for me. We'd gone to a museum that day and seen stuffed birds behind glass. Afterwards we fed actual sparrows while we drank in the park.

I managed to keep myself clothed. I could not approach my parents for money. It's just that I've never cared much for money. Money is not for me.

At the end of each lengthy night, I would wander into a diner where two men spoke a language that nobody spoke. The men gave me coffee for free. Sometimes a roll with ham. Whatever they said when they handed the cardboard cup over, I have no idea. But they said what they said with bright shiny holes for their eyes. Eyes black as buttons.

I'd walk back to my building through the billboards and grime, and climb up the stairs toward the small room that I rented.

But on the way there I'd first pass through the lobby where the manager sat, and I shrugged at him in greeting. He would shrug back, sitting behind a wall made of bullet-proof plastic in which was cut a hole. And through that hole you paid him. Often my payment consisted of coins that I'd found on the ground. If they did not amount to enough there were other arrangements.

He had a camera to keep an eye on trouble which often flared in the hallways. One of the cameras had a view into my room. If I lacked enough money I'd keep the door slightly open for him. The camera captured just shadows and sugges-tions of movement. These dark pieces of me seemed to please him. It is good because that was all there was to be given. And he took. He took from me. And I gave.

Each morning I would sit at my cardboard-box desk and open the cup of hot coffee. This meant peeling a small triangle off of the lid. This sliver of plastic I liked. I'd sip and then turn on the shower. I'd perch the cup on a shelf alongside the toilet. From the shower I smelled the beverage steam rise and mix with the steam that came off my body. I smelled of the city.

With the city washed off me I would lie down on the bed in ragged pajamas. They used to be white but had gone mutely grey. They once had flowers upon them. Yellow flowers with faces. I was glad they had faded.

Much to my own dismay then I would cry.

To shut myself up I trained my ear toward the hallway or down toward the curbside. I would hope very hard for a fight. I was lucky. All the time people shouted and yelled. At first the sounds made me suffer, but soon I realized that inside their exclamations was a message for me.

One morning, coming home for my daily rest, I first closed myself into the telephone booth in the lobby. I slipped coins in. I heard them drop into that well of metal. When my father picked up after three rings, I listened close to his voice saying "Hello?" and "Hello?" Then "Hello?" I hung up on him.

I started to do this daily.

In winter I called for the very last time. One freezing night a pigeon flew close to my face. Then it landed upon me. It sat on my shoulder and dug toes into my skin. Whispering, the bird stayed on my shoulder. I knew then that the world was ending. Yet I continued to walk the square nightly, and daily continued to sleep in my room. The bird slept on my windowsill.

With the pigeon whispering into my ear, I made quite a picture for the tourists in the square, despite my anger. I would hear them remark to each other: "She's from here." No, I tried to tell them with my eyes. Cockroaches, pigeons, and rats and mice. If the pigeon flies from my shoulder to yours, leave the city!

One night I wandered into an alley. This was on the coldest night I ever had known. Everything was dead, iced in the freezer of buildings, vaporized into thin slices of sky. I came upon a man even colder than myself. "I'm so angry," he said. I gave him my roll and my coffee. The coffee froze in his hand.

Then I passed a child inside a doorway. "My head is not thawing," she said. "Yes," I answered. "Mine is not too." She stared. I took off my jacket. She slipped her small limbs into the leather and disappeared.

Farther along, I came to another child. He had nothing upon him. You could see right through his skin. "Please, take what I'm wearing." I'd worn the pajamas all day and all night for ages—I was tired of them. So I dressed him. Helping his arms over his head and into my own grey pajamas, I remembered the dolls I'd had as a child, and how my mother had me. I reached for him but he ran away, the frayed edges of flannel fraying more on the street, his bare feet padding concrete.

At last I came to the river. The sun was starting to come up over the buildings on its other side. I turned to look back toward the city and saw the sun reflecting off windows, making bright eyes, and I thought about all the people who lived in the city, in their rooms and their alleys and hallways and bars, and I didn't know what they were trying to tell me with the lights they turned on and turned off and with the eyes the sun made on the building, the eyelids that blinked right at me. I knew it could mean nothing good. I began to lower myself into the river.

As I became just a piece of ice or garbage, everything dimmed. Through the dim light appeared stars, though morning was rising, and then the stars became nickels and fell to the ground. I lay on a slab and grabbed as many as I could in my palms. Then I crawled out of the river and on through the morning.

Back at my room, on the floor I called my bed, I clutched my nickels and fell asleep fast. And I dreamed for the very first time in ages: of birds that flew in glass coffins and children who flew inside birds. Everything beating.

When I woke in the evening, my hands were wet and clutching at nothing. The manager was sitting beside me and he lifted my arms, one by one, into the sleeves of a coat made of fur. He left the room after a while. And shut the door. I hugged the coat to my body and then recognized it.

With the seal so heavy upon me, I understood that all animals die.

I slept through the night and instead of climbing the stairs up in the morning, I climbed down and into the phone. I called my father. Then I sat in a chair in the lobby, wearing my seal. Together we waited as taxis drove past the window, like bees or the petals of flowers. I wondered which one was ours.

chapter four

On Merry's fifth birthday her braids reached her waist, and Mrs Gold tied them with black ribbons, her favorites. After attending a frightening movie about a young girl who had switched bodies with her mother, Merry received many presents. She tore open the boxes: a doll named Baby Alive (you fed her green liquid which then came out from her bottom); a toy oven that heated food with a light bulb, in which one could (Merry quickly surmised) bake paper dolls to see what would happen; and a sewing box, complete with rows of tiny spools of silk thread. Its scissors and needles were dull. Merry also got a red hand-knit poncho from her grandmother, with pom-poms attached. It itched.

Is it really any surprise that, after as many hours as she could stand fake-baking, fake-feeding and fake-sewing, all in a poncho that itched, Merry was bored? Even the doll's fake-pooping seemed dull.

In the evening, Merry snuck into Mr and Mrs Gold's bathroom and stood on the toilet while they enjoyed cocktails down in the den. Reaching for the windowsill, she foraged around for a blue plastic cup printed with an image of Snow White feeding birds, in which Mrs Gold kept nail scissors, tweezers, emery boards. Merry took the cup by the handle into her room where Ketzia slept, holding onto Baby Alive (Merry had given it to her after removing the limbs). With the nail scissors she gave the doll and her sister matching hair styles. It took a very long time, as the scissors would cut only tiny strands one at a time, but eventually, the doll and the sister had practically no hair at all atop their heads—just tufts of brown here and there, like orphans, or like girls sent to camps Merry had learned of in Temple.

Sitting on her bed, Merry leaned against the wall, which was newly papered with ballerinas she despised, especially their tutus that flared out. She twisted around and removed one of the tulle skirts, only to reveal nothing beneath—the ballerina torsos floated in air, and the feet floated below them. They were legless. Merry felt happy inside.

Happy birthday to you, happy birthday to you, you look like a monkey, and you smell like one too, she hummed under her breath toward her sister, although this wonderful birthday was hers.

chapter five

THE BEGGARWOMAN

O nce, when my sisters and brother and I were sitting by the fireplace and my mother was making us popcorn, the front doorbell rang. My father was away on business, so my mother walked to the front door and said with great suspicion, as she always did at a doorbell, "Who is it?"

My brother yelled from the den, "It's the plumber, I've come to fix the sink," which was from a show he liked about a caged bird.

You must have seen this old woman begging before? Well, then you can imagine who was there. The woman at the door begged, and when my mother gave her some popcorn she said "Thank you." She said, "Thank you" again. My mother shut the door upon her.

I marched right to that door, opened it wide and invited her in—not to be kind, but because it would anger my mother.

So the old woman joined us in the den and stood by the fire. My sisters and brother left for the kitchen, and the wind they made as they left licked the fire toward her rags. They started to burn, but she didn't know it. I stood there and watched, and I watched and watched. Now, I know I should have put out the fire. If I had no water, I should have wept so hard that a well flowed out from my eyes. Then I'd have had two nice little rivers to put out the fire. That would have been the natural thing.

Instead, the woman burned until nothing was left of her but a tiny black smudge.

When my sisters and brother and mother returned, they were all on portable phones with my father. They pointed and yelled and screamed. Of course, there was no trace of the beggar at all.

"She was never here," I said very loud. "You weirdos." It was an illusion, you see. But I had seen her, and she had seen me. What does that mean? Do you know, my pretties? Do you, my sweets?

Doch weh! Die Flamme faßt das Kleid,
Die Schürze brennt; es leuchtet weit.
Es brennt die Hand, es brennt das Haar,
Es brennt das ganze Kind sogar.

Und Minz und Maunz, die schreien
Gar jämmerlich zu zweien:
„Herbei! Herbei! Wer hilft geschwind?
Im Feuer steht das ganze Kind!
Miau! Mio! Miau! Mio!
Zu Hilf'! Das Kind brennt lichterloh!"

Verbrannt ist alles ganz und gar,
Das arme Kind mit Haut und Haar;
Ein Häuflein Asche bleibt allein
Und beide Schuh', so hübsch und fein.

Und Minz und Maunz, die kleinen,
Die sitzen da und weinen:
„Miau! Mio! Miau! Mio!
Wo sind die armen Eltern? Wo?"
Und ihre Tränen fließen
Wie's Bächlein auf den Wiesen.

"Then I'd Have Had Two Nice Little Rivers"

chapter six

S hortly after the birth of the fourth and last little Gold child, Merry spent the night at her best friend Becky's, across the street in a duplex. Becky Goldman had buck teeth, long blonde hair and often wore velvet dresses tied in the back with a bow. Her house was as dark as the Gold's house was light. Often, Becky wore a cast on a limb. Merry liked to tell Becky, "We have the same last name, except you are a man."

Merry dragged her suitcase up the Goldman's front stairs where snow—dirty soup, really, wet her feet and soaked the fringed bottom of her jeans. She wore wooden clogs with the name of a Swedish band etched onto the leather.

From upstairs in Becky's tiny, messy room, the girls looked toward the Golds' house and watched the figures move from room to room like dolls. Mrs Gold was putting Lucy to sleep, rocking her in a cradle. "Go to sleep, go to sleep, go to sleep my poor ugly," Merry sang.

Down the hall, Mr Gold read aloud to Ketzia and her brother. Ketzia had a floppy bonnet on her head and was tilting her head side to side as he read.

"My sister is stupid," Merry confided in Becky.

Becky opened her mouth.

"Are you stupid?" Merry asked Becky. "Do you breathe through your mouth, or through your nose?"

Merry returned to carefully cutting dolls from paper with scissors. She narrowed her eyes at Becky's unsteady hand, which was filling in drawings of clothing Merry had designed—a series of wedding dresses with trains that stood straight up high in the air, on which she planned to glue dead flies. Becky furiously scribbled white crayon onto the white paper, per Merry's directions.

Mrs Goldman came into the bedroom then, with a tray of food for their dinner: squares of meat from a can, triangles of crackers from a box, shreds of cheese from a bag.

"At my house," Merry said, "We eat hot food that comes in aluminum trays."

"Thanks!" Becky said. "Thanks Mommy!" Becky repeated.

"Creeps," Merry said, like she'd seen a girl say in a movie set in the desert.

Mrs Goldman stood by the window as the girls ate on the carpet. Across the street, Mr Gold read to two children—Lucy and her baby brother—dressed in flannel pajamas with feet attached. You could smell their shampoo over the decaying leaves out on the lawn.

chapter seven

MERRY KNOW NOT

In the suburbs, not far from the city but not right on the ocean, my parents raised a son and three daughters—Ketzia, Lucy, and me. The others were neither clever nor wise. And I was sharp as a needle, I don't know why.

Our parents slept late every Saturday morning, so we watched television for hours. I lay on the couch and ordered my sisters and brother around. Gesturing with my feet, I'd instruct them to change the channels. I commanded them to bring me toast. Frequently, I had my brother sit next to the couch so I could stretch my long legs onto his shoulders. He had a round head and sometimes I would rest my feet on that. Eventually I would send Lucy upstairs to wake up my mother. "Tell her she's slept long enough," I would say.

Always a day is unreal to me until my mother is making my breakfast.

I began, early on, to make demands of my parents. "I'd like my share of allowance for the entire year *today*," I said on the first of the year in sixth grade. We compromised on one month. My father thought it was a good agreement and that I showed signs of promise. He owned a firm. He did not know that the month's allowance bought me a bottle of peppermint schnapps.

In seventh grade, I asked for my allowance through college, but he declined. That was when I learned to find the money I needed. The easiest way was to barter with boys, though Ketzia I easily stole from. But boys were easy to please and their wants made them poignant; I felt sorry for them and I had no pity for Ketzia-who-only-annoyed. One shouldn't take money from those in need, but one may take it from those whom one pities. The boys were happy for favors; I know this much. And though I experience no happiness myself I have nothing against it in others.

In ninth grade, my parents left me in charge of my siblings when they went to a tropical island. As soon as my father drove onto the main street three blocks away—which I could see from my bedroom window, over the tops of oak trees—I shoved my brother, Ketzia, and Lucy into a closet. I hurried on my skateboard to town, went to the back door of the only bar, and exchanged the money my father had left us for drinks. When I got home, Ketzia and Lucy had put the baby to bed and were watching a television program about a family who lived on a farm. *Freaks*, I thought. I was too drunk to ask Ketzia and Lucy how they'd gotten out of the closet. I crawled into the closet myself.

I should have liked to stay in that closet forever, but my parents forced me into tenth grade.

There I finally became friends with the boy with the wooden leg. To my happiness he was not very nice, and we began having relations in a shed full of spiders. One day we were drinking peppermint schnapps and some other boys from school came in after he left. "What's your name?" they asked. "Jonquil," I said. "Touch-me-not, no name, no one." They could see who was in charge, I was certain.

Then some other things happened. They were not very nice to me, but not in a good way.

Soon after, at school my nickname became Merry No One. I heard some girls joking in the bathroom (which always had a wet floor) that the nickname meant Merry would sleep with anyone; so of course, I started to skip. I'd always suspected I preferred skunks, crows, and beetles to people. I'd rummage around in the woods for anything to talk to—cabbage, tree trunks, and mice. Some days I returned to the shed.

I began to take the streetcar downtown where I'd try to get drunk. There I'd meet students from the rich college. Those boys liked girls from the suburbs, especially Jewish girls for some reason. Their dorm bedrooms often contained nothing but an extra-long bed, a desk, and a lamp that bent like a neck. I don't know why—but I liked the lamp's bending.

Somehow my parents found out. That's when they sent me to design school in the city. I have no idea why. Maybe because I wore fashions, or liked to use scissors. In college there were endless parties.

There were also doctors, directors, and lawyers who paid to meet me in hotels. They gave me things I needed. Every morning I woke in a stupor, and drank pretty champagne from a bottle with an orange label.

One day I got tired and just said goodbye. I showed promise as a designer, but I quit—or perhaps I was expelled. Either way, I don't know why.

For a while I disappeared and then I slept in a hospital.

Later, I secured a position at a dressmaker's shop. There I traced patterns onto tissue paper, then cut them out. I pinned the tissue to fabric. There was relief in having nothing to do all day but trace, cut, and pin. This new life resembled a shelter for the deficient. I considered myself to be deficient. I was.

One day, a political figure—a great humanitarian many admired—came into the shop with his sons. Despite the father's position, all of their clothes were poorly designed, like fabric boxes for men. Yet the seamstress had instructed me to cut out identical patterns again. When she had left for the night, I tore the old suits apart, and made a far more fitting style. While I do not consider myself much of a humanitarian, preferring other animals to people, I do respect what he does, which is find homes for abandoned children. If it were nicer to live in the woods, okay, but it's not.

When the seamstress returned the next morning, she became angry. "What idiot did this?" she yelled.

"I know nothing," I answered, and held her gaze. I was sent to the back where I wasn't allowed to trace patterns. There my job was to dole tissue paper to the other girls.

When the three men came to pick up their suits, they were impressed. "I will bring great peace to the world in these suits!" the humanitarian proclaimed. My boss, the master seamstress, smiled. He invited her to dinner, and his sons invited two pretty girls who worked machines in the window. No one looked over to me. I returned to my table and doled out tissue paper until five o'clock, the last minute of work. I didn't come back.

I don't know why my experience with the humanitarian and the seamstress bothered me, but the following week I began a new job in the suburbs. In a small room with a fan that whirred on the ceiling, I took a brief test and aced it. The examination required me to trace a doll's pattern (one side Red Riding Hood, the other grandmother and wolf). I used to have a doll like that. One of my first childhood memories is of slowly lifting her skirt at the bottom of the stairs in the basement. But that is not why I aced the exam. I aced it because I have perfect vision.

Needless to say, the factory hired me on the spot. There is great demand for a girl who wants to make patterns, who doesn't get tired of that.

"One of My First Childhood Memories"

chapter eight

Like many young children, Merry had an infatuation with books; and books proved, in the end, her only forever-friends. From the ages of nine to eleven, she admired a trio of novels for girls, one about freaks, one about creeps, and one about weirdos. These were formative books; and after she'd finished the last of the three, all other books paled, and she became quite annoyed with print, save the small spiral notebooks she meticulously kept and the patterns for clothing she gathered.

In the notebooks she recorded every cent spent or earned. Mr Gold began to bring home Accounting Ledgers. He hoped that someday she would show an interest in management, perhaps at the family business.

Merry kept many notations in there. She recorded the number of times Mrs Gold tried to hug her; bacon slices her brother ate; newspapers Mr Gold read at the table; minutes Lucy practiced the tuba. *They don't know*, Merry thought, *but I have all the evidence.*

One night, during a long, two-girl bath with Ketzia, Merry took particular note of the number of photographs Mr Gold took of his wife. It seemed to be countless. He aimed the camera at Mrs Gold while she rinsed the girls' hair. Their mother looked very lovely. Bent over the tub, she turned her head from the lens. Was she shy?

Merry piled suds on her head to get her father's attention. "Look at me!" she shouted out standing fast. Bumping Mrs Gold's hand, she sent the soap flying high. Her father tripped, nearly fell, but one image was taken.

When Mr Gold picked up the pictures downtown, just as he did every Saturday morning, taking the kids along with him, Merry was dismayed that the clearest girl in the photo was Ketzia. Merry was just a blurry lump in the center. She took out her Accounting Ledger, and wrote "MINUS ONE" in the appropriate column.

Haughtily, Merry carried the ledger into Ken's Corner—where Mr Gold took them for hamburgers and sodas—and was careful not to put it down in a puddle of cola. Sitting in the window, they all counted joggers, a game Mr Gold himself had invented. The sisters got the women; Mr Gold and his son got the men. It would be difficult to accurately report who ever won, for Mr Gold always cheated on them.

chapter nine

I was lucky to be hired by Children's Clothing Company, also known as Triple C. The company had made a small—but lucrative—name for itself as a full-service provider of children's fashion, distributed through national department store chains. On my first day, I was required to memorize the words Correctness, Comfort, and Charm, representing the three company values for children's wear. When I inquired about *correctness* I was told it means appropriate elements of style.

My job kept me in a back room with the others, where all day we used our sharp scissors to cut shapes the designers had sketched, and then we'd pin them onto long sheets of fabric laid out in rows on wood tables. The designers would come check our patterns against their original sketches. Sometimes I made minor improvements that would remain imperceptible to the eye. Sometimes I left their sketches the same.

It was always cold in that room so we wore multiple sweaters, fingerless gloves, and knit caps. Bundled up this way it was as if we had no bodies inside. Nearby, the giant sewing machines hummed and whirred like a herd of seals on a rock; if you ever heard such a thing you'd know what I mean. It used to be that individual seamstresses made each item of clothing by hand, but now workers just tended machines—feeding in fabric and pulling out clothes. It felt like all of us together—machines and women—comprised a sort of giant animal, in fact.

It also felt like that in the automat where I ate lunch on my shift. You deposited a coin and a sandwich came out. I often selected cheese and tomato. Though I worked the swing shift, from three to eleven, our break was called lunch, even though most people, at that late hour, would be fixing supper. In the world of machines, things have different names.

My life was routine.

Each day, I awoke in the afternoon. I pulled on some brown slacks and a sweater, and took the bus to my job where I donned a blue smock. In winter an extra sweater, the fingerless gloves, and a cap. I stood at the table with pins everywhere. Snip and pin, snip and pin, pin and snip and snip and pin. Then the sandwich-eating, then snip and pin again. When my shift ended I removed my smock, took the bus home, and climbed in bed with my fairy tale book. Inside the front cover, I had drawn a column marked "Earnings" where I'd write in my wages, and a column marked "Spendings," where I'd write in the cost of my lunch. I'd read a story or two, and then fall asleep. Often I dreamed of machines, and also of dolls named Comfort, Correctness, and Charm.

I always awoke at the very same hour, the one of the star they call sun. I would check my limbs to be sure all were present, and checked my heart to be sure it beat.

One day at the automat, I chose to extract not a sandwich but a hard boiled egg. I put my hand around the cool oval luncheon. It was about the size of the hole in my head I imagined. I shook the salt in a rhythm, and ate.

chapter ten

MERRY, KETZIA, AND LUCY

O ften, Ketzia, Lucy, and I went to play in the woods by our house. The woods contained things that smelled good, like skunk cabbage and crows. When I turned ten, the city built a gravel path through it so people known as joggers could use it. These joggers wore foolish outfits in pastel colors, often with stripes down the sides of their arms and legs, as if to indicate "I am a member of Team Loser" to all. Occasionally, a man in yellow sneakers would expose himself from behind skunk cabbage, but more often to Ketzia than me.

The woods were forbidden.

I had organized many games for the sisters to play in the woods. All were based on a television program and book where the eldest daughter is sleeping in the loft of a barn and wakes up to discover she's blind. When she discovers she's blind, she suddenly forgets about fire, and knocks over a lantern beside her; as if she has also forgotten the motion of her limbs. Of course the barn burns down, despite all the buckets of water tossed at the barn by the whole town—or maybe just by her pa. No one gets angry at the blind girl, who is blonde and pretty and now has blank eyes.

In my game, the exact rules of which escape me at the moment, Lucy represented water, and Ketzia represented the fire and barn. I became blind and was known as Mary. We'd walk into the woods until we reached a creek (really just standing water that came out of a pipe). Then, I sent Lucy into the pipe, because she was small. "I now render you the source of the water," I'd say. Ketzia was forced to lie down in the creek, becoming the floor of the barn. I would hold my foot over her body and aim it just right, and then close my eyes. "I've gone blind! I've gone blind!" I would yell, and step onto her body. With some matches I'd swiped from home I would light one after another, and toss them forward. Then I'd tell Lucy to come out of the pipe.

"Why?" she would ask. I didn't know why! Poor Lucy, always wanting to reason.

Eventually I'd get Lucy to emerge and splash our sister with water. As she stood there, mud seemed to wrap itself around her ankles. And I liked the way she would look around for me then, as if I were going to argue with the mud on her behalf. By this time, Ketzia could barely muffle her tears. "Merry, get off me, you're breaking my back!" she wailed.

The game was over then, and Lucy would pick her way home with muddy feet. Ketzia would follow, crying and wet. And me? I would just laugh and laugh, standing there. I'd laugh so hard, I thought my head would split open. "Ha ha ha ha ha ha!" (Like I'd been smacked with an axe.)

chapter eleven

Readying the family for the annual Halloween outing, Mrs Gold applied Merry's makeup. This year, Merry had fashioned herself into a nightclub singer.

The dress was from a simple pattern: tube-style, slipped over the head. Off the body, it was approximately the length of a hand towel. Merry had attached a fake microphone to her cassette recorder, which was playing a song called "You Don't Bring Me Flowers," sung by a woman to whom people occasionally compared Merry's looks and demeanor.

This was the first year in five Merry would not be a bride. Although she tried not to show it, Mrs Gold's feelings were hurt. Privately she had been pleased that one of the girls had shown an interest in her profession. And she found Merry's alternative choice a bit dramatic: why must the child become a Harlot? But Mrs Gold always encouraged the girls to be whatever they wanted. "I like it," she said shyly to Merry, who showed no reaction.

Merry was quite disappointed in her costume. She was uncomfortable in the sequin dress; the sequins itched, the wool tights she had to wear underneath to quell the late-fall chill itched, and the microphone she wore around her neck was heavy and made her head hurt. All this was compounded when, walking downstairs to join the others, she passed Mr Gold on the stairs. "What are you going as, Merry, a clown?" he said.

"I hate you," she whispered to her face in the hall's mirror. No one could hear her.

Outside, waiting to climb into the car to drive to grandmother's for the annual Halloween photo, Merry turned to Ketzia. "What are you going as this year?" she asked. "A fat ugly devil?" (Ketzia wore a red leotard and red tights, intending to represent a cinnamon candy Mrs Gold ate to quit smoking.) Ketzia cried. She was easy.

In the back of the blue station wagon, on the way to their grandmother's house, Merry slouched, sneering. "Next year I'm going as a black cat," she said in a mean tone to no one.

Halloween sucks, she mouthed to the window, and watched as her breath made a mark on the window, a mark with a black hole in the middle.

chapter twelve

"The Crumbs on the Table"

The rooster once said to his chicks: "Quick, come in and pick the crumbs off the table. Your mistress has gone visiting." "No, no," said the chicks. "We won't do it. The mistress would beat us." "She won't know," said the rooster. "Come on. You know she never gives you anything good." "No, no," the chicks said again. "Nothing doing, we won't do it." But the rooster gave them no peace until they finally went up on the table and started picking up breadcrumbs like mad. Just then the mistress came in, grabbed a stick and gave them a good dusting. Once they were outside, the chicks said to the rooster: "Did you see see see see see?" The rooster laughed and said "Didn't I know know know?" Then they ran away.

chapter thirteen

Though it may seem peculiar for someone raised by a manager to work in a factory, I do. My father managed a factory where people stood by machines and by him. He was a good manager and everyone liked him. So in that way I was inspired to be a good worker. I saw that being properly managed could be a wonderful thing.

"There's nothing wrong with working in a factory," I often say to my sister Lucy.

"I never said that there was," she always replies. It used to be *she* was frightened of me.

"Ketzia works as a typist," I add. It is a great shock to discover myself aligned with the sister I always have shunned.

And my mother—whom I expected to approve of such a feminine trade—often asks me when I'll return to my so-called art. "Sewing is an art," I answer. "Even in a factory." As if to mock my achievements, she keeps my old sketches framed on the walls. In the kitchen, above the beaten-up wooden table, is a drawing of three pigs in bonnets.

I simply don't think one ought to question one's own mode of employment too much. I like the day-to-day tasks at Triple C. They suit me.

And besides, this is what happened. This is. Once, I was young and made fantastical dresses. Then I had problems. I became an Apprentice Seamstress instead. And, though I had a rather unpleasant, short-lived promotion as a pattern-maker—no need for details—I remain an Apprentice Seamstress. These are the facts. What happened matches what is. I like things to fit.

Also, when I realize the difference between the designers and me—they merely make ideas while I make dresses, I realize the true dread of their existence. I live in pins, fabric, and needles—and also inside their visions. Their dreams are the pincushion I am.

It is difficult to explain to people who have not learned my trade, which involves precision of thought and of feeling, that it does have its own kind of despair: for I make tiny patterns on paper as thin as onion-skin.

Regardless, today, as on all Fridays, I have made a roast chicken for dinner, just like my mother on Sabbath. I dressed the bird with onions and stuffing, and shook garlic salt over the breast. I trussed the feet with twine, put a dollop of shortening on top, and placed it in the center of a very hot oven. There it will sit for three hours. It is important to foster a feeling of home even if one lives alone. Even if one never achieves the position of Master Seamstress.

chapter fourteen

DEATH PAYS A VISIT TO MERRY

One morning, when I still lived in the city, I walked through the meat district on my way home from a party. A stranger stepped out of the alley and said "Hey, Miss—"

"Excuse me?" I answered. I was never afraid. "Mr Weakling," I thought in my brain.

The man was smallish—good looking. "Do what I say," he said, "and you'll have a chance to live." But I refused. What a joke! He took a step toward me and then the two of us fought. And though I was drunk I won easily. He seemed not even to be trying. I hit him one last time on the side of his head with my palm, and left him in the alley. Exhilarating.

But all the next day I couldn't sleep—quite a rarity. I kept thinking of him. Dragging myself out of bed in the light, I went to the zoo in the park, to visit the monkeys. I can't stand people, particularly in daylight, but other primates, they don't bother me much. I wanted to ask the zookeeper if he had any dead monkeys I could use for my sewing.

What I wanted, in particular, were tiny ones to make miniature negligees for, but apparently there are city regulations for corpses. No matter, the live monkeys were good company for me. Perhaps I was still a little bit lit. I sat on a bench.

Soon a young man walked by me, humming a song about swimming at night, a lullaby I remembered from childhood. I hoped he'd overlook me and keep going past. It seemed every time I went out, freaks would assault me, as if I possessed a phantom limb they wanted back.

But he sat down beside me.

He was thin, in corduroy pants and long underwear. His hair stood straight up on his head as if he'd been touched by a light bulb. Even I could only shake my head and laugh. "Don't you recognize me?" he said.

"No," I replied, "I prefer not to know you."

"I'm the guy from last night," he continued. "I've been looking for you. I want to give you my card." He pressed it into my hand and then he was gone.

I looked at his card and shuddered. It was printed in letterpress script. On the back, written in pencil, was Lucy's name. What a strange coincidence, don't you think? I crumpled it up.

This was in February, which was windy and cold. Soon after, my health began to fail. I don't know if someone sold me something bad or what, but I felt ill all the time, and nothing but vodka could calm my stomach. I had the bottles delivered from the place down my street. The messengers brought one carton a week. Sometimes I'd drink a whole bottle all at once, in a very long swallow.

Finally I reached the end of my luck. They refused to deliver more bottles, and because I was angry I threw all my empties out the window and onto the street. I got arrested.

Or perhaps I am making that up.

Anyway, I don't know who took me there, but I ended up in the hospital and attached to machines. I cried for the first time in decades. I begged the doctors and nurses to leave me alone. But they wouldn't speak at all.

After a few weeks that same guy showed up. "I'm going to tell you something, so listen," he said. "You black out every night. Do you sleep? Do you dream? Do you even stitch? You lie on the floor as if you were dead. And don't you know that people want you to live?"

That last one really upset me. He got no reply, I tell you. I'd made my bed. I wasn't afraid to lie in it. Resigning myself, I closed my eyes and fell asleep after some nun put liquid in my arm.

When I awoke what I believe now to be many nights later, I hoped that young man would be there. Instead, I saw an official from school along with my parents.

So I'd been kicked out. It hardly mattered to me. They set me up with a sewing position; I was to be working strictly from patterns. "That's fine," I said. I like to work.

Something they gave me in the hospital must have altered my brain. I've heard things they have now can do that, without even electric shock. A chemical to the head, and you're gone.

Fine.

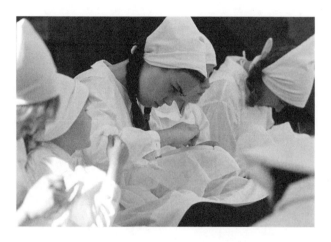

"Working Strictly from Patterns"

chapter fifteen

I find I am able to live a very wholesome life now, one that does not make me fearful or mad. Recently I moved from the city into a small house in a town, on what is known as a "lane." It is really more a half-circle than a road. Lacking of sidewalks! And all of the houses have identical shapes: small and rectangular, with two little eyes for their windows and a chimney on top like a hat.

I spend all my time here, leaving only for work at Triple C.

Ah, the suburbs. I've found that living somewhere that reminds me of childhood is important to me. Why? There are, I have learned, theories that say childhood is far more vivid than any experience one could have later in life. Seeing, feeling, smelling, hearing, and tasting in childhood reach the level of depravity, this theory says.

Some call this rapture, others bliss. I cannot say that my depravity has ever reached the level of happiness, but I do find that when my life is as orderly as it was at home, I am closest to fine.

Yes. Reproduction is what I want.

In fact, my next-door neighbor has three daughters, just like my mother did. The girls resemble each other so strongly that you can barely tell them apart. I often bring them identical outfits I make in my free time at work (one pattern, three sizes). Today, as they played in the lane with their mother, I noticed they wore the green corduroy pants, yellow smocks, and pink hats I had fashioned. I made their outfits with gardening in mind; they represent Flowers.

Out of my window, I watch their mother prepare the dirt for some plantings. She appears to have bought some flats of daisies, marigolds, pansies.

In honor of their gardening, for lunch I prepare myself a simple dish called Flower Soup, which is chicken broth in which one floats slices of radishes and carrots. Children greatly enjoy this soup. My mother told me that she used to make it when we planted flowers growing up, but my mother never gardened. What a lie!

I tell the neighbor-girls every day to be happy. If their parents ask me to baby-sit while they go out to eat steak or see a movie, I read the girls fairy tales before bed. These stories have different houses in them, all sorts: cottages with chimney-hats, castles with moats, homes where children sleep in the stove, huts with hedgehogs hidden in corners, houses on bird-feet that spin in the woods.

Live now little ones! I sing to them.

chapter sixteen

MERRY TAKES A LITTLE SLAP

My grandmother used to tell me all sorts of stories, and they all began exactly the same. *Amol iz giben.* She could be mean, like I was, but she was only mean in secret, away from my parents. In a way, this I admired.

For example, one time she was lying in my mother's bed. My parents had gone to Florida to take in some sun. Everyone else was asleep, but because I was the oldest I got to stay up and watch the late shows with grandmother. As she got ready for bed, she let me watch her undress. Standing in her slip, she pointed to herself and said *"Amol iz giben.* See what you have to look forward to? This." Then she leaned forward and gave me a peek. *"Oy,"* she said. "I'm ready to go. *Oy,* I'm ready to die! Merry, why do we live so long? Lord help me, He should take you away before you reach eighty." I ran to my room to get away from her sighing. Weeping is a weakness and it would make me less strong, it would make my skin melt, like grandmother's.

Once, when I was a baby I became afraid when my parents left her to stay in our house. I remember crying and crying. I was the only one born yet of the four kids. She came over to the cradle and rocked me a while, but then she gave me a light slap which made me stop crying.

Another time, when I was older, I felt ill. I was sitting at the kitchen table. She wore a floral housedress and smoked. The smoke made me sicker. On the television, there was a tiny lady sitting in a giant rocking chair, talking in a baby's voice. At the sight of her I started to cry. "I don't feel well!" I said. "So spit up," my grandmother said, resuming her smoking. I ran to my room and cried some more.

And when I was still older, and she thought I was sleeping, many times I watched her sneaking through the house, out to the garage. She trotted up to a dusty cupboard where a flask of brandy was stored—or a bottle of spiced rum someone had brought my mother as a gift, covered in dust—I was too young to know liquor, but it was something like that. She would take out the brandy or spiced rum and have a few sips, then she would add some water to the bottle and run back to bed. She was like a rat in the wall, or a shadow slivering out from under a door.

Every time she stayed with us, my grandmother drank from the bottle, and no matter how much she poured out, it always was full when my parents returned. It's a trick I learned to use later. At first, my mother never noticed that the bottle was less dusty upon her return from some trip. She only cared that the level stayed the same. But when I got older, my mother knew all about my little problem.

Still, *amol iz giben*, I got away with a lot.

chapter seventeen

Merry stood on the brick path between the house and the garage with her sisters and brother, all in bare feet and cut-off shorts. They ate candy and waited for their grandfather to set the camera on a tripod. Merry had a handful of chocolate babies in her palm. Carefully, she bit off their heads with her teeth, putting the torsos in her pocket for later.

It was midday in summer and the sun made the brick path hot. This reminded Merry of a story her grandmother had told her when she was a much smaller child.

Winters in Russia were cold. The winters in Russia were so cold that her grandmother's mother would heat rocks in the oven for grandmother to carry to school in her pockets, to keep her warm. Later, when they moved to America, her daughter, Merry's mother, was very thin. On Weigh Days at school the young Mrs Gold would carry rocks in her pockets so she wouldn't have to eat liver. The story began with rocks and ended with rocks. To Merry it was perfect somehow.

Merry fingered the babies in her shorts pocket, and thought about how they wouldn't add much to the scale, nor would they keep her warm. Yet, without their heads, they would frighten Ketzia, who got hysterical at the sight of de-capitation—paper dolls, stuffed animals, bugs. And Merry liked to pop the legs off dead spiders, leaving only the head, which also made Ketzia insane. What was the pleasure?

For now, a short anecdote must suffice. On the hot, summer day, Merry's grandfather had set up his camera and sheet. The Gold children and their cousins would now perform in a play called Disappearing Act, which was very involved: first, Merry would stand behind the sheet, and then the camera would begin running; her grandfather would lift up the sheet and there she would be. Next, the camera was turned off and Merry would run, and when the camera was turned on, *voila*! A lift of the sheet. The girl was gone.

This was repeated with Ketzia, and Lucy, and then their brother. Next, the two city cousins and another cousin, a luminous orphan. Being oldest, Merry would get to perform one more time. In this spectacular finale, when the camera was turned back on it would reveal not a missing, but rather a nude girl!

This final segment, curiously, was called Disappearing Act too.

chapter eighteen

The Ice Girl

One day, my parents were sitting at dinner with us children, and a good friend—Danilo—came over to visit my father. It was very late. Normally, the children ate dinner as early as four o'clock in the winter, just as soon as it got dark. After dinner in winter, my mother would persuade us it was nearly midnight and put us in pajamas and shoo us to bed. I would kneel on my bed and stare out the window, where, when it had snowed, the light would glow a bright, white, bluish color for many hours, and keep me awake. In summer, it was more difficult for my mother to banish us to bed, as it stayed light until very late indeed.

This night, the night Danilo came over, it was summer. It was past ten o'clock when he arrived. We were at the round kitchen table eating hamburgers and fries. The fries had come out of a plastic bag in the freezer. I liked eating them when they were still frozen. They made my teeth ache pleasantly. I liked it especially in summer when the air was thick as honey. You had to swipe the air from your face. On summer nights, the bees went away but the sweet heaviness remained. Only ice could fix it.

Danilo was my younger sister's guitar teacher, and my

piano instructor. Often he would drop by at night—striding in from the mudroom, through the kitchen and straight into the den. My father would follow. They'd shut the door and speak in hushed tones. He'd leave as quickly as he had come.

I would go into the music room when he was there and play the piano. I was learning songs that were scary; they had names like "Music Box Dancer" and "Tiny Dancer." Danilo made the selections for me.

Danilo taught his lessons in the Academie Musicale, a huge stone building on a wooded hill, across from Bullocks Pond, which froze in winter. Danilo's teaching room was a dark room you reached by stepping through its doorway and walking down a long, narrow hall. Every time I went for piano, another girl left just as I would arrive. She'd practically run past me down the hall, weeping. Sometimes she wore a fancy dress that was white. It had a pink satin bow. I wore bell-bottomed jeans and sweaters with stripes. "Who's that?" I asked Danilo, whenever I'd see her. He never answered. I'd ask again, and again be ignored.

Over time I began to ask to play the same songs she played (I could hear them through the door as I waited before my lesson). She played creepy songs too—songs with creepy lyrics and creepy sounds and creepy names: songs called "Haven't Got Time for The Pain" and "Guess I Just Lost My Head."

In winter, the lesson room was freezing. Often my teeth would chatter to the rhythm of the music. Snow blasted against the window outside. I was a skinny, chattering doll in a freezer. Gay piano music bounced off the walls. I felt I inhabited a movie or a cartoon.

At least it feels that way now.

Although I was supposed to be learning piano, often Danilo would play piano himself, and have me dance around the room. After a while I never did play. I suppose I played very badly and he got tired of me. Also, when I would try to play I would get so nervous I'd hold my breath and pass out and fall off the bench to the floor.

"Dance like a butterfly," he would say. "Dance like a bird." Because the songs were so creepy, the dances I did were creepy too.

When I was done, Danilo would have me sit on the bench and lean my head on his shoulder until our time together was over.

I remember being exhausted. I remember seeing my face stare back at me from the black window. I remember the shiver of cold on my spine. Sometimes snow would blow into the room and cover our bodies.

And it was strange: even though my father gave me money to pay Danilo, Danilo never would take it. "Keep the ten," he'd say. Or, "Keep the twenty." Never did he once take the money. "I won't tell on you, if you won't tell on me," he would say. I'd shove the money deep in my pocket. Sometimes I would leave the Academie early and walk down the street to a fried chicken shop, and order potatoes with gravy, sometimes a leg. I always had the urge to eat the chicken under the table. Something about my piano lessons made me feel wild, untamed.

Once, I was leaving my lesson and as I climbed into my father's car outside the Academie Musicale, I saw the little girl in the white dress across the street, on Bullocks Pond.

She was walking on ice. While I watched, she picked up a thick stick and started hitting the ice. She looked right at me. Then the ice opened up and she vanished.

"Dad! Dad!" I screamed, pointing.

But my father saw nothing at all. "You're just tired." He patted my head, a rare show of affection.

I shoved his hand away. "In the ice," I muttered. "The ice."

"Damn it, Merry!" he exclaimed.

The girl was never at her lesson after that night.

"Where is she?" I asked Danilo, even though I knew she was gone.

"Hm?" he would answer.

"*The ice walker*," I yelled one time. "Where is she? IS THE ICE WALKER HERE?"

Never any reply.

When spring came that year, and the pond's ice-cover melted, I kept expecting the town police to find her body. I remember a series of headlines in the newspaper, too: "Little Girl's Dress Found on Bullocks Pond," "Missing Children Files Scoured," "No Skating Next Winter: Bullocks Too Thin." But they didn't find a girl's body.

I soon noted that Danilo started taking my father's money. In fact, I reported this to the Police Department in an anonymous letter I mailed from the post box outside my school. "My piano teacher, who works across from Bullocks Pond where a girl might have disappeared, has begun taking payment for lessons!" I typed with my mother's electronic keyboard.

Dissolutely, I continued piano with Danilo. But during my lessons, he no longer had me dance, and he no longer had me rest my head on his shoulder. Ketzia had started lessons by then and he seemed to prefer her. She glowed like a firefly after their lessons. Me, he'd just have play scales over and over again. Soon I quit going. Making sounds was never for me. (This could be why, when I do speak, it comes out sounding angry.)

Oh, I'd still take my father's money and pretend to go to my lessons, but instead of getting fried chicken I'd buy cigarettes and smoke them out by the Pond. Danilo never told.

I have few memories of all this, which does sometimes create a disturbance, a layer of dissatisfaction. "On thin ice," is how people describe it.

This is why I live alone and dislike friendship.

Recently, I was visiting home for Christmas. As my mother and I went to pick up a freshly killed turkey at the farm, we swung past Bullocks Pond in the car. I swiveled around in my seat. The surface of the pond was covered in ice and mist; and even from inside the car I could hear the snakes and toads and leeches sleeping in cold mud.

"Remember when that girl I knew drowned under the ice?" I said a little too loudly.

"Don't be ridiculous, Merry. That pond is *polluted*," she said. "It stopped freezing before you were born."

I narrowed my eyes out the window.

Ever since then, I won't even let ice in my drinks. Yet strangely, despite my great dislike of ice, I am a very cold person inside!

This is different from being unkind.

chapter nineteen

Down the basement stairs crept Merry, while her sister sat underneath them, waiting for punishment. Today it would be extreme. Though the exact origins of The Punish remained unclear, the game was of Merry's design and was based on at least three precise sources: a magazine she had seen at her grandfather's house about an orphan and some men (in one picture they stretched her legs with ropes); films from Temple Shalom of girls' heads getting shaved; and a dramatic exercise she and her best friend invented, during which one played a nurse injured in war and the other a soldier administering cures. These were combined into The Punish by Merry who played as Sir.

Today, Merry planned to be particularly cruel to Ketzia, who cried at the slightest hint of disapproval. Sometimes, Ketzia cried so easily—so quickly—that the game was ruined. What fun was it to punish someone who suffered so quickly? The point, Merry often tried to explain, was to *suffer in silent gratitude for being left alive*. If Ketzia played it right, Sir would feel remorse and smother her with kisses. Other times, Sir withdrew from the basement to join The Deserving World, leaving Ketzia to think about what she must have done to make him so mad.

Because Sir was unpredictable, Merry told Ketzia, Ketzia should behave in as predictable a manner as possible. "The trick to survival," she told Ketzia, "is to remain calm and follow orders. If orders are followed, there *is* a chance you will not die."

Today, as Merry stepped down the stairs, she felt no joy at the awareness of her sister cowering below. If she could think of a better game, a game that would make her feel alive, she would play it with fierce concentration. Instead, she could only muster the most dutiful, scolding tone at the sight of her skinny, unimaginative sister who could only obey. That was no fun. She stared dispassionately into the dark basement, with its red rug and black walls and darkroom and sinks, and wondered "Why am I here? Am I so mad?"

Shaking the thought out of her head, she picked a spider off Ketzia's leg and held it in front of her sister's mouth, just to see what would happen. Imagine Merry's surprise when Ketzia opened her mouth and defiantly ate it! That was a shock.

Merry ran up the stairs, unnerved by Ketzia's bold action, by her sister's chomping. Though all she had desired was for Ketzia to do something, anything strong, she was disturbed about not being in charge. And why did she have to be so mean?

Upstairs, she frantically clapped hands with their younger sister Lucy, who was always happy to engage in games, lifted straight off the playground or from the TV—she was easy, Lucy; she followed the rules without fear—though she did have a temper. Merry had deemed long ago that Lucy needed no training like Ketzia.

Merry and Lucy sang about flowers and then reached the part where you only hummed. It was tiresome, but filled the time. "Hm hm hm hm-hm-hm-hm," they sang, as Mrs Gold prepared supper, a meatloaf smothered in ketchup. Bloody Meat, Merry called it, just to upset her mother.

chapter twenty

MERRY'S BALLAD

Once upon a time a young girl
Left her home. Her name was Merry Gold.
She planned to roam till she was old,
 And she was gone for many years.
Merry sinned, and almost died,
And so God told her: "You're too bold!"
"That's how I'm made," Merry replied.

Years later, the girl came home disguised
So well she was unrecognized.
(She knew how to sew, and had devised
A costume out of hide.)
"Mrs Gold, tell me, say,
Have you fine clothes and do you stray?
And tell me, tell me, do you sin?
Do you lust for other men?"

"We've no fine clothes, we do not sin.
I do not lust for other men.
Why do you wear so much fur?
You remind me of another girl."

Mrs Gold wore rings so bright
She took them off most every night.
They were not silver, they were not gold
But they were bright and very old.

"If you give me rings to wear,
I'll tell you secrets, if you swear
Not to repeat them, ever, hear?"
Merry, in her fur, said to Mrs Gold.
"I will not take these off, my dear.
They're for my daughters, they don't live near.

If you knew them, you would see
Why those two girls are so precious to me."
She didn't look in Merry's eyes.
She did not see past the girl's disguise.

And so Merry turned away.

As she walked down the brick path,
Merry said with a small laugh:
"I thank thee, Mother, with this kiss,
And I thank God for wordless bliss."

Merry's mother was quite stunned
When she felt that kiss come from her;
And Merry stood in sealskin fur,
And waved goodbye.

chapter twenty-one

THE CHINESE ROBE

Long ago I reached the end of my luck, and now I frequently think about vodka.

Yet one time, when I was enrolled in The School of Design, the world held much promise for me. Of course, like many insolent girls, I wanted nothing to do with my classes. I preferred to stay up all night, to sleep all day.

I lived in an enormous city in a tiny apartment which made me feel like a mouse in the wall. So, like a mouse, I took what I wanted and always left a mess for someone else to clean up. Only occasionally did I go to school where I was learning to make patterns and sew.

In high school I had done nothing but scissor my clothes and staple them back together, just to worry my parents. They encouraged me to apply to the School of Design. I agreed, for the School was in a city well known for its parties.

Once there, I immediately made two beautiful friends, Semyon and Tibor. They made everything sparkle. With them, I felt understood for the very first time. Semyon and Tibor completed my patterns, and I completed their own.

With great ease I began to win prize after prize at school for my work: skirts made of rose branches, pants sewn of apple peel. And before leaving my apartment each night to go out, I would make us new get-ups. I dressed Semyon and Tibor in whirly-gig pants, with ants in cages as earrings (we placed bits of leaves in so they wouldn't go hungry); I would have used butterflies but I never saw these in the city, though once I saw a dragonfly as big as a pigeon fall from the sky.

We spent nights at burlesque nightclubs, in back rooms you entered by making friends with lovely women who grew beards. The rooms were guarded fiercely. You got let in through a heavy red velvet rope.

Because we slept by day and roamed by night, winters were tiring, the days too short to catch up on sleep. So it came as no surprise to me that by January, I was far behind in school. That would be the end of my parents taking care of me, I knew. So I asked Semyon and Tibor to help me catch up. I had a final project due, in a class called "The Question of Fur." Semyon had made a coat with a big lion-mane hat; Tibor some infants' caps by decapitating stuffed animals and gutting them: monkeys, lions, and dogs. Myself, I had designed human-hair sweaters for frogs. I'd had my brother send me dead frogs he found in the countryside where he lived. Then I shellacked them.

As I expected, the boys were happy to sit around and thread the hair I'd gathered on my own comb for months. Of course I fed and entertained them while they worked, as usual—with carrot and celery sticks and elaborate dancing. I pretended to whip the boys with a snakeskin scarf I'd designed. In public I was very sullen, even cruel, but in private, with my friends, I felt wild.

Little by little, as we sewed hair into sweaters, the conversation began to turn on the subject of who, among us, was meanest. We were each mean in our own special ways—Tibor liked gossip; Semyon slept with people and then never called them; but my meanness was harder to define. It was perhaps that I felt so profoundly mean, the meanness didn't have to manifest itself at all.

Semyon said, "Merry's not afraid of anything, which makes her the meanest." I was surprised when Tibor agreed. O my Secret was kept!

"So," Semyon said, "go down the street and buy me some drugs." He was killing himself, but Tibor and I did not know how to stop him.

"I will," I answered, "but in the meantime, don't stop sewing the frog-clothes for me." Back then I never missed an opportunity to let others do my work.

I went down to the street. Children swarmed out of the alleys and crept along the walk like a pack of mongrel puppies. They handed me tiny cellophane packets.

As I went back to my apartment, I passed a narrow alley where a fragile girl was fast asleep. She emanated, in her vulnerability, every single thing in the world I was striving to hide. Lying on a cardboard box, she wore a Chinese robe my favorite color—black embroidered with snakes. I shook her shoulder but she didn't wake. Maybe she wasn't even alive. I poked her again, then slipped the robe off her back and put it on mine.

Quickly, I walked home—and as I entered my fancy building I saw a man on a couch in the lobby. The couch was made of white feathers and he folded his arms in their black leather sleeves. He made me think of a panther settling in with its prey, a loving affair in its own natural way. I ran for the stairway.

"As a reward for myself I took this robe off a girl," I said, coming in the door. Tibor refused to believe it, and Semyon made no expression at all. I felt their disapproval, which only made me feel meaner.

"Sew," I said, "sew."

They kept faithfully sewing. After a long time, they piled into my bed and fell asleep. I sat staring at the tiny hair sweaters. They were gorgeous, just as I had imagined.

I watched Semyon and Tibor sleeping. Together they made a helpless four-legged creature. I tried one of the sweaters on a frog and propped the frog on my knee. "Do you know that you're dead?" I asked it. The lights of the city were just going off as the sun rose. I hugged the silk robe to my body; it was the most beautiful thing I ever had seen, perhaps the only beautiful thing I ever had seen.

Finally I fell asleep. But soon there was a knock at the window. The alley girl stood on the fire escape. "Give me back my robe," she whispered. I took the robe off my back and went to the window.

"No," the girl said. "Bring it back to where you got it." Her voice was thin as a snake's. She disappeared. Suddenly the traffic started speeding up below, with that roar of a city.

We slept all day, as usual.

The next night, the boys had gone back to their own apartments, and I was left alone with my needles and hair. I didn't have enough for the stupid project and had started to take them off of my head, from underneath where no one would notice. The girl came again to the window. "Give me back my beautiful robe," she said. I went to the window, and took off the robe and stood there naked. "No," she said. "Bring it back to where you took it." She stayed there during the quietest part of the night refusing to take it out of my hand. And as soon as the traffic started again, she vanished.

The next night, at the very same time, there was a loud rap on the door. I looked through the peephole expecting to see the lovely thin girl.

Instead I saw the man from the lobby. "Give me my money," he said.

"Who the hell are you?" I shouted.

He pushed the door in with his shoulder. "Give me the money," he said. He walked around the apartment—if you could call it around. The apartment was small as a shoebox. He picked up one of the hair sweaters and held it up to his nose. He smiled slowly with an animal gleam in his eye. In return, I held my nose at the scent of his leather jacket.

It turned out Semyon owed him an enormous amount of money for drugs. After performing various services, I got him to leave Semyon alone. Semyon and Tibor were my only true friends in the world.

The next morning I had to get up and go to class. It was either that or fail, and then my parents wouldn't pay the tuition. I put the three little sweaters into a bag. In another, I put three of the deadest frogs you ever have seen. At school I would dress them. In my own way, I was proud of this project, though the assignment was Fur and I had used hair.

But when I got to class, the room was empty. I saw some words scrawled on the blackboard telling everyone to go to assembly. Resentfully, I went to the building next door where a famous architect had designed a modern auditorium. Other auditoriums have a raised platform as a stage, but this one had a huge glass cube inside of which performers would stand.

That day, inside the cube stood a priest and the college president. A lot of students were crying. The girl with the robe was sitting beside me. "Semyon is dead," she whispered. Someone began to sing and then a terrible wind came up. Everyone shivered at the very same time, except for me. I remained perfectly still. Through the air Tibor came rushing toward me, pale as a ghost, and the air that he traveled entered my body and seized me. And then there was no air, only the girl from the alley. The silk of her robe filled my mouth.

Somehow I slipped out of the service unnoticed. I never returned to my classes. And that is why, to this day, I never make friends. Not a one.

That part of my story was done.

Sing every one,
My story is done,
And look! round the house
There runs a little mouse,
The that can catch her before she scampers in,
May make himself a very very large fur-cap
                        out of her skin.

chapter twenty-two

THE STOLEN PENNIES

One day a man was sitting at the dinner table with his wife and children and a good friend who had come to visit them. As they were sitting there, the clock struck twelve. Just then the visitor saw the door open and a pale child in snow-white clothes came in. The child didn't look around and didn't speak but went straight into the next room. After a while it came back, passed through the room as silently as before, and went away. The second and third day the child came and went again. Finally the visitor asked the father whose child it was that went into the next room at noon every day. "I didn't see it," he said. "I have no idea whose child it might be."

When the child came again the next day, the visitor tried to point it out to the father, but he didn't see it, and the mother and children didn't see anything either. The visitor stood up, went to the door of the next room, opened it a little and looked in. He saw the child sitting on the ground, digging its fingers into the cracks between the floor boards and looking for something. But when the child caught sight of the visitor, it vanished. The visitor told the others what he had seen and described the child. Then the mother knew who it was, and said: "Oh dear, it's my darling child who died four weeks ago." They ripped up the floor boards and found two pennies the mother had once given the child for a poor man, but the child had thought: "I'll buy myself a piece of cake instead," and had kept the pennies and hidden them under the floor boards. But it had known no peace in its grave and had come back every day at noon to look for the pennies. The parents gave the money to a poor man and after that the child never came back.

chapter twenty-three

Merry Comes Back

After I failed school and completed my time in the hospital, I went home for the holidays. The leaves had all fallen from the trees when I arrived. This made me angry, for I had expected at the very least to catch a glimpse of the season. After all, in the city, the only leaves we had on trees were fake ones; the city had decided it was a good idea to place metal trees along the boulevards, fake-planted in dirt.

When I stepped off the train I was wearing what I considered to be a smart outfit, a grey woolen suit with a jacket and skirt, black pumps, and my hair loose and curled. Lucy met me there and though I had taken great pains to look right I saw her face fall. "Merry, Merry, what have you done?" she asked. Her hair was straight as a pin. She had gotten it ironed. For some reason my family hated curls. We were encouraged to have them flattened.

"I was grazing horses," I answered, making no sense.

Lucy rolled her eyes. She was always so practical. "Horses," she said. "Right." She took my valise and we left the station in my mother's new car. The color of a robin's egg, it gleamed.

When we got to the dead-end on which we'd grown up,

I looked all over the house for my mother. "Where's Ma?" I asked my brother, who was in the den with our dad.

"She went to the market," he said. He gave me a giant grin—always so kind.

"I heard the market was flooded," I said.

My father looked up from his chair. "Merry," he said with complete aggravation. "What are you talking about?"

"I drank it," I said. "I did."

"Um," Lucy began, and then left the room.

I sat down on the couch beside my brother and watched large men fight on television. I folded my hands in my lap. Lining the wall were many pictures of me—in pigtails and braids. I could see in my eyes that I'd always been wicked.

"Did you sew that outfit yourself?" my brother asked.

"Yes," I said. "Before the worms got it…" my voice trailed off.

"Always trying to be so different," my father remarked.

"No," I said. "I don't want to be different at all. I work hard, really hard, at my job." I was becoming depressed. Outside the sky was too blue; inside the walls were too brown. I walked to the back of the house and looked out to the woods. There were oaks there, and maples, and a few dying pines. But where are the acorns? I thought.

When my mother came back home we sat down for our supper, and I behaved very well. I figured I owed them.

But all that night, in my childhood bedroom, I lay shaking awake.

chapter twenty-four

"Once upon a time," I read to myself, "there was a princess whose name was Water." This was in an old picture book of my mother's about a girl who dries up in summer drought. It always makes me cry, but not unhealthily. In the modern world too, people disappear. It is just a fact.

For example, recently Triple C got a big contract with a Parisian chain of stores. This necessitates that my boss go on frequent trips to choose fabrics. Though I miss him when he's gone (as surely does his wife), I don't much care for the selections he makes, all of which have pastel animals with smiling faces on them. Animals on clothing, particularly underpants, give me the creeps. Certainly, I tell him, there must be more beautiful fabric—blue flowers, violet stars.

Now that he occasionally visits me for affection, it feels to me that I am living in a fairy tale or book of paper dolls. Or in a favorite book about a dollhouse family, where the mother was lit on fire and melted. Or a book about a girl made of water.

When I was a very young child, I would wake my dolls up, three-in-a-row in their pink dollhouse bedroom. I'd dress and send them to school. They'd come home and eat dinner, hear a story, and go to sleep. Then, I would line up three outfits in three different sizes, on three little chairs in their room; I myself sewed these outfits. I would take out three little bowls for cereal—thimbles—and set them on the table with three little spoons by their sides, real spoons my mother had bought me at the dollhouse store called Goulding's. My girls never would leave me for I had removed their legs.

If I had no legs, I would wear long flowered dresses that trailed to the floor from my wheelchair. Now, in the evenings, I sit outside on a lawn chair and marvel at the order, the design, which surrounds me.

Looking toward the houses on our lane, I tick off small differences just for the record: a front light on here, off there; a geranium at the end of our driveway, and at the end of our neighbor's, a succulent plant. There seem to be, on average, three differences per house. The houses are ranch-style with brick exteriors, with identically shaped lawns and driveways.

Something about the summer air and the order on my lane restores me. Other people make me disappear. This is why I am working so painstakingly to sew little characters from stories—the girl made of water, the boy made of air. They need clothes so that you can see them. They need me to make them real.

chapter twenty-five

LUCY AND MERRY

Once, for a brief time, my sister Lucy and I kept house together. This was upstate, in a cold winter climate. Together we made ice wine—we fermented it ourselves in antique jelly jars. Sometimes when we would boil the jars to sanitize them I would get scalded. I never minded, but Lucy did.

"Why are you yelling at me?" I would ask her.

"Don't you have any feelings?" she'd reply, clattering the jars and pot on the stove. Then she would take up a broom and sweep, sweep, sweep.

Sometimes, just to get away from Lucy I would go outside and run in the snow. I had a big pile of clothes I had made for classes and would wear everything: woolen pants, knitted sweaters, furry caps. I had a huge scarf I had sewn out of old shirts of our father's, and I'd wrap it around my neck again and again until no air could touch my skin. Then I'd open the front door, which was in the kitchen, and run and run.

"Where are you going, Merry?" Lucy would ask, standing in the doorway freezing. She always wore fashionable clothing—even in degrees-below-zero. She'd stand there and shiver and refuse to go in until I answered.

In a circle I'd be running.

"Don't I have cause enough to make patterns?" I would ask her. "I've collapsed on a sidewalk, woken up in a hospital, and now been sent here to live with *you*. I can't even scald my own fingers." Oh, I was angry.

Finally one time, I had run so long in the snow that I got down to the grass, and that wasn't easy: it had snowed nearly six feet that winter. The grass was flattened and brown, an inversion of living. "Now see what you've made me do?" I asked Lucy. "I've made holes in the snow, I've made holes."

For days I would get down on my knees and try to fill the holes, but they always showed—O O O. Somehow they haunted me. I imagined myself curled up in each one like a huge snowflake. Oversized things had always repelled me. Not only that, but if I was a giant snowflake the sun could not fail to burn me...

Needless to say, we kept house together for a very short time.

One night I was up late, darning my woolen socks. They were brown, striped with pink. I imagined a family of mice at my feet, peering up and watching me sew. "Thank you for keeping me company," I said.

"You're welcome," they answered. They nuzzled my legs, and then they sang. They sang of the world and how it was ending.

I felt rapture as I gazed upon them. So I was unhappy when I saw Lucy staring from the doorway. Some things are terribly private.

"I'm going to have to ask you to leave," she said. She looked cautious. I could describe her even as frightened. She was not a particularly timid girl—not like Ketzia—and so this surprised me. It wasn't the first time I'd been kicked out of somewhere, but I decided it would be my last.

"Fine," I said. "But in that case, I'm going to have to smash this." I threw the little jar of ice wine I had been drinking down on the floor. Soon I was sobbing furiously, and in my mind I saw everything buried in snow: my sister, her broom, the mice.

The next day I too disappeared.

"They Sang of the World and How It Was Ending"

chapter twenty-six

The photographs in the attic—which seemed to only horrify her younger sister and brother—fascinated Merry. Certainly their being forbidden lent appeal. And then there was the female body, growing hair where it did not belong. Like animals with hides.

For Merry the magazines she and Ketzia found in pink suitcases in the dusty attic of her grandfather became the raw material for several theatrical productions of which she was costume designer. These had themes of animals and love, a sort of fairy tale with no happy ending.

Digging in the cruise trunks that were also up there, Merry found silk dresses, feather boas, men's tuxedos, wool bathing trunks, hats. Cutting them with huge scissors from Grandpa's study, Merry made them into costumes for scenes lifted from the magazines and blended with other, more familiar, stories. Calling a small audience—usually Lucy, and their younger brother—Merry and Ketzia would act out stories.

One favorite of their brother's was a tale about two girls in cowboy hats who rode a man like a horse. The sisters wore cardboard hats, which Merry folded and stapled, and boots which they found in the attic—high heeled, with stars drawn upon them in crayon. Ketzia played the horse with little argument, pleased to be included. Merry and Lucy perched on her, naked but for the cardboard cowboy hats and the boots. How their brother laughed at this! How he laughed!

The most elaborate staging Merry ever produced was based on a cartoon strip featuring a girl in a red dress with saucer eyes that never closed. To this day, thinking of the cartoon she feels queasy. The girl stood in a field of grass surrounded by men. In the next frame she was shown hung between two trees with rope. The men looked up her dress. The girl's mouth was open with a look of surprise—but also, Merry thought, without hope. And so were her eyes.

chapter twenty-seven

THE NAUGHTY LITTLE MERRY

O nce upon a time there was an old lady who lived all alone at the edge of the woods. Everyone knew that if you entered her house you would never get out.

Sometimes an old man stood in the old lady's backyard yelling "Hester! Hester!" It was confusing because Hester was also the name of a girl in a book we read at school, and the name of a street in a movie where Jews lived in an apartment house, one family on top of the other. I had seen the movie in a noisy theatre with my mother's best friend, Auntie Perfect. I confused the Jewish families with dollhouse families sent to be punished at camps. This confusion, along with many others, went uncorrected.

I'm not saying my head worked right, but I am saying that everything—the old man in the yard, the woman who lived alone, the tenement house, the dollhouses, camps— made me very mad. As a result I behaved unpleasantly, and would not obey my mother at all, and enjoyed teasing my younger sister until she would cry. I'm not saying I'm proud of any of this. But it is how I felt.

One day, I told everyone at school that Ketzia had only recently been let out of an institution where she had been plugged in the head with electrical wires. It is true that Ketzia had been taken away because she was sad, but it is not true that they plugged her with wires. However, I found myself extremely jealous that my parents cared enough to take her to the hospital, for I was sad too.

Though one day I also would benefit from being tied up in a white smock, my mind then was full of wicked thoughts. I was held up for blame, though there was no truth that I had bad intentions. I had no choice in the matter.

I simply came forward and told all the truth. The teachers, the students, the bus driver, and the cafeteria lady, all learned that my younger sister's head was full of electricity and to keep away from her.

My parents chose to banish me from the house without any supper that night. I deserved the punishment, I will admit. But still, I felt bitter and forlorn, and I skulked in the neighborhood yards, behind ranch houses, the smell of chicken wafting from all. Finally, I traipsed into the yard of the woman known as Hester, at the edge of the woods. From a hole in the screen door, her bony arm reached out and beckoned to me.

The old man stood at the edge of the yard and watched. Once inside I saw him turn around and around. As he spun, our dog Hansel ran up the road to him from my parents' and asked "Old man, why are you turning?"

"What difference does it make?" he answered.

Hansel started turning around and around too, and along came my youngest sister, Lucy. "Hey old man, hey Hansel, why are you turning like that?"

They said "What difference does it make?" and Lucy joined them.

Next came a chickadee. "Hey man, hey Hansel, hey Lucy, why are you turning like that?"

"Why don't you turn too?" they all replied. The bony old lady and I watched as the chickadee, with its black and white cap, joined them. *Chick-a-dee-dee-dee*, and they all sang along.

I hardly could stand it. *This is exactly what I mean*, I said to Hester, but she was gone. It was eerie and frightening in her house alone, but I was distracted by the commotion outside. A bit of pitch and a pin had come along and the man, the dog, the girl, the chickadee, and the bit of pitch and a pin were all spinning around on the lady's lawn. I couldn't believe my stamina for staying away from home so long, but eventually night fell and it was time to go to sleep.

Since Hester was gone, I invited all of the spinners in, and they took their places. The man lay down in the bed, my dog lay down in the cradle, Lucy put her head in the oven, the chickadee flew up the chimney, the pitch went into a box of long matches and the pin, unable to find anywhere else, stuck himself in the hem of my skirt.

They all got quiet. I was alone. But not for long: from a trap door in the ceiling, Hester emerged from the attic, insisting that I go to bed, up there, with her. She said it would keep her warm because her husband was dead. So we went to the bed—of course, I was frightened, and wished that I was good like my sisters and liked it at home. When we got to the bed, the man kicked out at us and scared the woman so that she sprang away. She then tried to lie down in the cradle, but Hansel was there. He bit her, quite unlike him. The old woman dragged me by the hand to the oven, opened the door, and Lucy walked out.

"Woe is me," wept Hester. "What's going on in my house?" She tried to light a match to see what was the matter, but the pitch stuck to her hand so badly that she could only clumsily reach for the hem of my skirt to wipe her tears. Then, the pin pricked her so hard she fell on the floor.

The chickadee said, in its sweet little voice, "Witch-a-dee-dee-dee," and at that, the old woman was so terrified that she dropped dead on the spot.

I saw all of this. It entered my head through the holes of my eyes. I never told a soul, not a one. But I will tell you this: I ran all the way home, chasing fast after Lucy and Hansel-the-dog, never once looking back to Hester's. And for a while after that I did everything my mother told me to do. I scrubbed the tub with a talc named Comet, vacuumed my bright blue shag, and spoke to my sister at school.

chapter twenty-eight

This job keeps me absorbed, a state that I currently cherish. I find great comfort in such quiet inside-conditions which allow me to draw the correct paths for needles and pins.

Because I am now the only patternmaker for such a large company I must work fast, and to work accurately I must contain my movements within a small sphere. I must waste no time or muscle; patternmaking takes great precision.

The seamstresses don't have the luxury of interpretation; they must simply sew and not stray from the lines I have drawn. Since I have worked as a seamstress I can assure you that a daydreaming seamstress is inefficient indeed. And those drawing the designs must forever mine their own dreams for forms. I, on the other hand, can interpret my dreams freely, without letting on what I desire.

A patternmaker has great control over the flow of images to her brain, and control over how she shapes them onto the page.

There are a few drawbacks. The most obvious is that one's fingers get cramped. A second is that the designers are hoity-toity. I like nothing worse than a phony. But I can match their coldness with indifference. In the past, I was a rather icy person. Though I no longer hold enough attachments to humans to be cold toward them, I am able to remain blank in their presence. This suffices to deal with designers.

Finally, the seamstresses leave me alone. A patternmaker is above a seamstress, after all—not that I care about rank. Of course, we are all susceptible to replacement by machines. This brings us closer, or should.

There are some who, like my parents, worry that I've wasted my talents. Wasted my talents? I scoff. I'm a superior maker of patterns! I've been promoted! This is my gift. Just so. I see forms by day; and by night, I trace pictures from fairy tale books I keep by my bed. This keeps me quiet, this makes me feel whole.

chapter twenty-nine

THE SUN WILL BRING MERRY TO LIGHT

During my troubled days as a student of design, I would sometimes take my creations to shopkeepers, hoping to sell them for money. But it seemed few people had interest in Lepidoptery Skirts and Cocoon Berets. So I was utterly destitute.

One hungry day, walking down an avenue with not a single penny for food, I saw a man dressed in traditional religious clothing. I banished Good from my heart, and demanded he give me his money. I said, "Hand over your wallet or I'll put a curse on your life!" I was dressed in one of my designs—little mice made from fur lined my collar and cuffs and the hem of my skirt. Certainly a curse did not seem out of the question.

"Please, spare me my life," the religious man said. "I only have eight pennies."

I narrowed my eyes to see if he was telling the truth. He was not.

"You've got money," I said to him, "and I'm going to get it." Inside my heart I willed that the man become weak and perhaps take me home. I imagined his house to be full of dark, polished wood and in the oven, a roasting chicken, and there would be three children there, dressed in wool clothing. They would be quiet children, not like my noisy siblings, and they would put me to bed and stroke my arms till I slept.

I wavered on my feet.

"The bright sun will bring you to light," the religious man said, and then he himself fainted. I found this peculiar since I was the one who was starving.

I glanced around to see if anyone was looking, and then I crouched to the ground and felt in his pockets. Indeed! Only eight pennies! With that neither he nor I could buy even a green pickle. I helped him to his feet and placed him to rest on a bench beside the spindliest tree on the street.

Two years later, I had lost everything—my degree in design, my two best friends Semyon and Tibor, my parents' affection—and I sat in the subsidized lobby each morning. I always sat on the same couch by a window and watched the people go by. I watched them go into a bar where they sold drinks of pomegranate. I watched the world live while I stared.

Sometimes an old man who also lived there would bring me a cup of coffee, and on this very day, what do you know? He did.

Some of the coffee dribbled onto the saucer, out of the cup, and I held up the saucer to sip it. I was about to pour it down my throat when the sun shone on the coffee, casting a reflection that danced and made rings. "The sun is trying to bring me to light," I cried out.

"Dear girl," said the old man, whom I considered a friend, "what are you talking about? What do you mean?" Usually I only spoke of the weather, and of my wish for some needles and thread.

"I cannot tell you," I answered.

But he replied, "If you love me, you must tell." He spoke ever so sweetly and gave me no peace. And so I told him the story: how years before, at a time when I was hungry and penniless, I had stared at a religious man and brought upon him a curse, and before the man fainted, brought down by that curse, he spoke the words: "The bright sun will bring you to light."

"Just now," I went on, "the bright sun danced on the wall and made rings, but that's as far as it got." I implored him not to tell a soul, and he promised. We in the subsidized housing were loyal to one another.

But after I began darning my sweater he went to see a special friend, an old woman who had lived down the hall from him for many years. He told her the story in strictest confidence, but before even three days had passed she had told everyone in the building and from then on all residents averted their eyes from me. Whether in the elevator or in the lobby or on the front stoop, I was sentenced to that death of being alone.

So the sun had brought it to light after all.

chapter thirty

"UPON ME"

There once was a noblewoman who had a large estate, and in a hut in one of her woods an old woman lived. She was a lonely old woman who had no relatives and who lived on what bits of cooked and baked food the rich woman gave her. But the old woman never said humbly, "Thank you my Lady." And this bothered the noblewoman. How could a person be so ungrateful as never to say thank you?

She thought about it. "I'll teach her the difference between 'mine' and 'yours,'" she decided. So she baked a large handsome braided loaf of white bread, a *koyletsh*, into which she put poison. When the old woman came, the lady gave her the loaf. The old woman was so pleased by the size and quality of the loaf that this time she said twice, "May the Lord repay you, my Lady." And went away. When she was gone the Lady burst out laughing. "We'll see whom he repays!"

The old woman meanwhile, when she got home, was so pleased with the loaf that she decided to hide it. A little while later the Lady's son was hunting in the forest and was caught in the rain. Remembering that there was an old woman who lived in a hut nearby, he ran to it.

The old woman was so delighted to see him that she took the hidden loaf out so that she could treat him with it. When he had eaten of the loaf he felt very sick. The old woman was frightened and ran to the Lady's house. "Lady, what have you done? What misfortune have you brought down upon me?"

The Lady understood at once what had happened and said, "Upon me. Upon me."

chapter thirty-one

There are days, as one might expect, when I lose all passion for sewing. My fingers go slack at the pencil and pins. It is at these times I listen to the drone of the sewing machines as one listens to a beautiful symphony that has lost its meaning.

There used to be a symphony I often played on my stereo when in a bleak mood. Its grey tone and slow swell stitched securely to my feelings.

But some years ago, when I placed the needle to the record and heard the music begin I felt nothing. My insides appeared to have drained. It is difficult to say why.

Now, I'd be the first to admit that among my life's achievements, emotional depth would not appear. But, during my many years of employment at Triple C, I had experienced at least one emotion with great delight. Let's call it grey. Grey was a relief in contrast to bitter or cold, though I believe *coldness* is underrated.

Grey, however, has a wonderful texture. For example, during romantic encounters with men, one may drift as in a fog or lovely mist surrounding a castle. This is far better than thrashing or fighting with them! I can concoct this pleasing grey feeling with even the most casual of strangers.

That is, I can bring this wordless fog painlessly upon myself as one can only otherwise do if sent to the surgeon. It's simple: when I lose my desire to execute garments, I seek someone out and lie down with him. I enter the mist.

But if too long a time passes between episodes, I find that my mind wanders unpleasantly at work. I have trouble interpreting instructions and put three arms instead of two; or I forget to make a hole for the head. I have to retrace and retrace merely to get a garment correct on the page.

Yet with some small violence to myself—an internal slap on the cheek, 'who do you think you are, little miss seamstress'—I get back into my mode of employment.

chapter thirty-two

THE THREE SISTERS

For a long time my sisters and I argued over which of us was the cleverest, strongest, and most deserving of our mother's affection. We argued and argued and none of us would give in to the others. Finally we decided to settle the matter in this way. "Let us lie down to sleep," we said, "and whichever of us wakes up and reaches our mother first will be considered the cleverest, strongest, and most deserving of her affection."

So I lay down to sleep and so did Ketzia and Lucy.

In the middle of the night Ketzia rose quietly and ran away from us, choosing a short road to our mother's room down the hallway. There she became nervous and started to weep.

Lucy, upon waking, walked toward our mother's room neither too slowly nor too fast, but just as a daughter should walk.

And I? I overtook them both with such force in the hallway that they became frightened. They begged me and begged me to take them in my arms and carry them to our mother. What can I say? I did. I wasn't always so awful.

Nevertheless, it is still me who wakes first in the spring and rouses our mother from her long winter sleep.

chapter thirty-three

Merry was a fearsome child who spoke clearly and confidently, forcefully expressing demands, and for this reason it was seldom suspected that she harbored any secret wishes darker than those she so wantonly expressed. But no one in the Gold family knew what Merry knew, which was that all humans are missing a part of themselves—and Merry could tell which.

The little lame neighbor was easy enough: though to most people it appeared that his most blatant absence consisted of a flesh-made leg (replaced with that wooden stick), Merry saw he harbored a bigger secret under his skin. The boy liked missing that limb. What was missing in him was the desire to fit. For this reason Merry and the boy exchanged knowing glances.

Ketzia, Merry knew, suspected she was missing a lot, and the poor girl was right. Such insecurity! Oh dear. But Merry knew, as Ketzia did not, that what was missing from her was neither strength nor confidence; rather, it was acceptance of being sad, no more depth than that. Merry only came to this understanding later in life, but in childhood she knew how to look at her sister and make her wither, as with a spell.

Ketzia appeared, as most children in that suburb did, normal enough, stuffed with peanut butter, corned beef, *tsimmes*, and bread.

Out of this special vision emerged Merry's desire to sew. While other kids enjoyed sports or reading, Merry liked the machine that stitched threads and whirred. It struck her as a miraculous electrical animal, one that could make an entire creature itself—in any shape, the essence of *hamburger* or *child* or *dog*. And to Merry it was essence that mattered, not flesh that filled one in—or thus failed.

She worked her way methodically through the three-ringed instructional guide Mrs Gold got her, with its wonderful titles and confident tone. *Do Wonders with Sewing, The Inside Personality, Secrets of Shaping, An Open and Shut Story, Save By Sewing Children's Clothes.*

The children's clothes chapter interested Merry the most, yet it had an ominous size chart, listing *Girls*, *Boys*, and *Husky*.

This list of words scared her; this list would scare anyone.

chapter thirty-four

I find that factory-work suits me not only when at my wooden table at Triple C but also when home in my studio apartment, where I also maintain a work-table.

Because I do not have friendships, I am able to practice my workmanship all of the time. In this day of machines, a seamstress, in order to remain useful, must expand her abilities beyond the mundane. That is, in addition to executing designers' conceptions, a talented seamstress will also invent some conceptions of her own—in private. Keep her vision alert.

For this reason I offer myself exercises. This year, I have been working my way through a troubling book called *Flower Children*, executing the costumes shown in its pages. The drawings are flat, containing few colors, and the clothing is drawn in broad strokes. This leaves much room for me to imagine precisely, and I take care in selecting the fabric swatches (which I take from extras at work).

This week, I have been working on a blue frock for a figure three inches in height, with green felt shoes and a blue-and-green cap:

> *Morning Glory thinks it's fun*

> *To wake as early as the sun,*
> *But long before Old Sol is gone*
> *You'll find she put her nightie on.*

My little sister sent me the book as a gift, saying that a guy she had dated had gotten it for her and she could not stand to have it around. Poor Ketzia, always abandoned by men. I have no such problem for all that I need is air. That reminds me of another poem:

> *I like to think about the air*
> *It is so very queer;*
> *It is around us everywhere*
> *All through the atmosphere.*

There was a time when I did need more.

Once, for example, I invited a supervisor from Triple C to my apartment, to show him the flower clothing I make. I had an idea that he might wish me to present it at a company meeting. He laughed at the outfits—orange skirts for snapdragon; pale pink for peony—they gave him pleasure, I saw. But then he gave me a curious stare and walked out the door. I suppose he went home. At work, after that, nary a word.

I find there are many who do not understand my particular passion for sewing. And perhaps it *is* strange: I find even a lone stitch meticulously placed to be erotic.

If I found anyone who did share this passion, I would certainly live with that person in peaceful union! Daily we could walk to Triple C with our hot morning coffee in a mutual thermos. Side-by-side we'd sit at our tables and trace lines onto paper.

And at night, side-by-side we would sleep.

chapter thirty-five

MERRY'S PLAN

Once there was a girl who had talent, but she became a beggar and dropped out of school. Both the girl and the beggar were me, Merry.

Listen to me. I didn't want to be a beggar, but life left few options. That's how it seemed. About all of this, I find it difficult to speak.

It was sad to drink vodka all day. To try to get away from myself, I would walk in the city among nicely dressed people: musicians, bankers, fishmongers, lovely paramours.

All averted their eyes. Dressed in the tatters of outfits I'd made at the School of Design years before, I probably scared them. I'd pair a knee-length woolen skirt with a shirt made of feathers, or a pantsuit with a monkey-fur stole, but something was off—something always ripped, soiled, or smelled. I knew this; I was ashamed.

But I needed my vodka and I could not work—I could not think to work—nothing could enter my mind except the cold flow of liquor. Without it I felt I would perish. And so every day for vodka I searched.

One day I walked along a busy street full of cars. This was not an extraordinary sight in the city, but that day it struck me as evil. The cars lined up against each other, hot and breathing it seemed. I wended my way through them, frightened. Admittedly it did seem often to me during this time that anything I encountered, whether animal or machine, comprised a horrible threat. That day it was all I could do to keep myself from punching the cars with my fist. And when I walked past a spectacular woman, I wanted to slap her face—I'm not proud to admit this. In the past, people had told me I looked *stunning*. "Not a traditional beauty," they would say with approval. But that was before the vodka.

It is surprising but on that dark day in the city, I joined forces with someone else. He was another beggar, a handsome young man. He began walking with me at a single-digit street and we kept going till we reached threes. The whole way we pretended we were husband and wife. I don't know how it happened; it did. He wore a t-shirt on which it said "Ay-li-lu-lyu" and American jeans. I wore a t-shirt on which I'd embroidered some hummingbirds.

"Do you have any vodka?" I asked him.

"I don't, but I will ask for some when we reach the next neighborhood."

"And I will ask for some olives to put in it," I said.

But then the man grabbed me and began to beat me, saying "Don't put olives in the vodka, it will get tart! Don't put olives in the vodka, it will get tart!"

Well, when we got to the next neighborhood, no one gave us vodka. And who can blame them?

I've wasted so much of my life. I hate myself.

chapter thirty-six

"THE BLADDER, THE STRAW, AND THE SHOE"

A bladder, a blade of straw, and a shoe went to chop wood in the forest. They came to a river and did not know how to cross it. The shoe said to the bladder: "Bladder, let us swim across it on you." The bladder said: "No, shoe, let the straw blade instead stretch itself from shore to shore, and we will walk over it." The blade of straw stretched itself across the water; the shoe walked on it and the straw broke. The shoe fell into the water, and the bladder laughed and laughed until it burst.

chapter thirty-seven

The kitchenette cottage the Golds rented each summer at the shore wore its name in big black letters over the door: THE FLOATING SHORE. Mrs Gold drove from the suburb to the shore with the children while Mr Gold stayed home to work, arriving for weekends. The hot little cottage had four rooms and an attic, and a bathroom shower painted blue; it rattled like thunder and its walls peeled. Whenever Merry took a shower she liked to peel as much sky-blue paint from its walls as she could, while the entire room filled with steam and the sound of harsh weather.

Merry stood in the shower now, feeling sand between her toes and tasting the last remnants of crumbs in her mouth from her lunch—bologna and cheese on white bread with mayonnaise. Thinking of her little sister she winced; they shared a bedroom with knotty pine walls, from which you could scrape sap with your nails, and at night, the room would fill with the breath of Ketzia. Why was it that the hot room filled with her sister's breath, and not with her own?

Mrs Gold often told Merry that she was mean, and perhaps this was the reason; perhaps—though the words Merry used in her head weren't those—perhaps when she felt mean inside, the breath that came out was different. She breathed in the shower to experiment with this. Standing in front of the mirror with blue paint under her nails and sand in her toes and the smell of bologna, she breathed onto the mirror, itself covered in steam.

Merry's wet braids—she couldn't be bothered with washing her hair—clung to her neck like the seaweed she had earlier hung there. In the sea, unlike in the school or temple or home or car, Merry felt best. There she became as beautiful and mysterious as some magical creature, able to frolic and play. Under the water, one didn't breathe in but only breathed out; and the breath proved that you lived on this dark giant planet.

And when you rose out of the water with a long, deep green seaweed-boa covering your shoulders and head, your sister screamed. And this was good. But in the bathroom of THE FLOATING SHORE, with only wet hair on her back and the breath-smell of bologna, Merry cried—why?

"In the Sea She Became as Beautiful and
Mysterious as Some Magical Creature."

chapter thirty-eight

MERRY'S GLASS

When I was in school—that briefest time—when the night sky glittered and even the stars were all black—I had two friends who loved me. Semyon and Tibor and I did everything together.

And our lives were laden with wine. We had wine so often we lived in it. We each had our favorite kind: Semyon liked red, deep as what lived in your veins; Tibor liked golden, with bubbles, need I explain? And I was happiest with wine that was faded between: an imperfect almost-pink.

We drank and we drank, and we sewed.

For a long time we each drank the same but then my drinking sped up. I drank faster and faster. I don't know why.

After a while, when we gathered for bottles of gold and sparkling pink, I couldn't go out when we were done. Semyon and Tibor would go to the parties and bars.

They left me alone.

One day, between them in the hallway, I noticed a kiss.

This small speck of happiness they together enjoyed—it could not be so! They loved each other more than me.

I stared and stared through the peephole in the door, a tiny hole that sent my eye into a tunnel through which no one looking in could see. I looked into the picture of them making love to each other in the hallway and how the fluorescent light lit them beautifully, like some kind of joke. I hate jokes; jokes are the opposite of light, and it was light that I wanted.

Their love was perfect. I gave up then. And a lot of bad things soon happened. Some of the misfortunes involved funerals and hospitals and others involved debasing myself in various manners.

Suffice it to say that eventually I had no friends on earth, and only my parents to rely on. Yet, I had disappointed them so much that their disappointment inhabited me like a second body. Of course they still took me in for a while, just as they'd taken in Ketzia during her barren seasons.

I hated my life and everything in it, and I hated everyone on the planet—or rather every human. My love for coneflower, aster, buttercup, wheat: that never has swerved. Hedgehog, otter, turtle, snake. Damselfly, newt, and bat.

Once, when I was living with my parents in my room with its blue shag carpet and white doughnut-shaped telephone, a man flew into the window at night. Often I dreamed of a man sneaking into my room at night, a peasant man with bags and carpets and blankets piled upon his back. That man would lurch toward me in the dark and wish to do me harm. But this man who flew into my room reminded me of the man who'd once yelled at me in the park. That was before the hospital, I think.

It had been a long time since any friend had called upon me. I begged them by letter, I begged them by phone, but they never came round. I felt like a wild animal kept in that blue-shagged room. I would peer out the window all day and all night. I heard many years later that the neighborhood children were frightened of me and called me The Window Witch.

So this man flying in through the window, well! You can quite imagine he was welcomed by me.

And I could see what sort of trouble he was in. It must have been terrible if he was bothering to fly into *my* room in the night.

"I'm tired and thirsty," he said. "Could you give me a glass for my wine?"

"I would gladly," I said, "but I have no glass." Clearly he was not in the mood for conversation. Yet, I was not allowed glasses in my room. Nor scissors nor needles nor thread. Out of a vase by my bed, on the space-age night table I'd had since my youth, I picked a marigold. I handed it to the fly-ing-in man.

"I used to go to bed when the sun rose in the sky," I said to him. "And now I go to bed when it sleeps and rise weep-ing."

He dunked the flower in wine, and put it to my lips. I drank it. Then he flew from the room. The wine tasted bit-ter and made me retch and the flower flew from my mouth, blooming like illness.

That was the last glass from which I ever did drink wine. And my parents still call it Merry's glass, I think.

"The Marigold That Goes to Bed with the Sun,
and with Him Rises Weeping."

chapter thirty-nine

I'm a very good seamstress, I feel. I know where to sew, where not to sew, and what kind of sewing never to use. Oversewing, I feel, ruins as many clothes as sewing carelessly. And, though I am now employed as a seamstress, I used to be responsible for patterns. Those days are over, but I believe that one must be expert at both in order to be successful at either.

However, I fear there has been much slackening in the profession. Some of this is undoubtedly due to the increased use of machines; some is due to the low status of such employment, not to mention low pay; but I have found a small niche at Triple C and find that I do best within modest means—it keeps my brain lucid.

I should admit a certain pride in the fact that during the rougher years of my past, I became used to living in meager government housing. I got used to being alone. I know how to make a vacant place home.

I can't say it's a wonderful life but I can say that I know how to live it. For example, I know how to make do with a hot-plate, and a sink that sits next to a bed. This provides convenience: I can wash my face in the morning without even rising.

The one trouble is that I find that my mind wanders too freely sometimes, unless I keep it on patterns. If I had recognized this when I was younger, I might have avoided a great deal of pain.

These days I focus on my employment. The newest line at Triple C is one of matching outfits for children and their companions—generally stuffed animals or humanlike dolls. I have been given the task of putting these into miniature patterns simply to see if they'll work. So today I draw a pink frock, not unlike Cinderella's after the rags, for a creature the size of a mouse. Triple C hopes to introduce these fairy tales into its winter line.

I do lament, at a time like this, the fact that I no longer design. I quite like the idea of children dressing in aprons and burlap and wooden shoes. Instead, children will be persuaded to wear lace dresses, tinsel crowns, clear slippers—or worse.

Of course there is great solace in the fact that whatever concoction the designers dream up and describe—waving their arms dramatically and smiling with unbridled conceit—it is still I who retires to the table in the windowless office, takes out the needle, and sews.

A stitch in time saves nine, after all.

chapter forty

The Water Nixie

Before our brother and youngest sister were born, Ketzia and I were playing near a well in my parents' backyard. Before the others arrived we had no one but each other. Though I was not fond of my sister, we got along.

We assumed this one was a wishing well and would spend hours gazing into it, pretending to pull up and let down a bucket of water and making a wish—we confused getting water with wishing, or believed them related. And perhaps they were!

The reason I believe this is because one day, when we were playing near the well, and we pretended to pull water up in an invisible bucket, I wished that something bad would happen to Ketzia. And as I watched, she fell down the well in her pink leotard and black tights. She'd just come from ballet. How I hated her toe shoes. And now they were gone.

I glanced back at the house where inside my mother cooked supper and waited for Dad to come home. What could I tell them when they realized Ketzia was gone? I became a bit anxious, but soon the glee of her going convulsed me with a delicate shiver I had never experienced before. The yellow house glowed in the evening and was trying to tell me something.

Then the wish went wrong, for I fell in too. It had always seemed that anything bad that happened to Ketzia happened to me as well, but I had hoped this would be different since it was my wish, after all.

So imagine my horror when I found myself below with Ketzia in her pink leotard. And my horror only increased when I felt comfort seeing her there—despite myself, I was scared!

Down below, there was a water nixie, who said "Now I've got you, and I'm going to make you work for me." She led us away toward the edge of her land.

She gave Ketzia an axe with which to chop down a tree, and pointed to one of our favorite maples. It had grown in front of our house since we were born, and I had gathered its whirly-gigs for many years. How had it gotten down in the well? I was glad that the axe my little sister was given was very blunt, for she hit and hit the tree over and over again and never a dent in the bark.

The water nixie gave me some nasty tangled string to spin; I made a cat's cradle from it.

Some other things happened that I will not relate.

Of course, the only food the water nixie fed us were dumplings. My mother and grandmother made dumplings every Friday but these were much worse; while my grandmother's were fluffy, left in the fridge to rise all day, the water nixie's were hard as rocks. They weren't even made from *matzoh*. It seemed they were made out of sand.

Finally, after what seemed to be many days and nights, the nixie went to church. We ran and ran as far as we could.

Ketzia, usually so meek, grabbed some tall grass and tossed it over her head. The grass grew into a hill with thousands and thousands of thorns, and the nixie didn't get over it fast, but she finally succeeded.

I reached into the back pocket of my dungarees and pulled out a comb, and winged it over my head. It grew into a hill with thousands of teeth. But the nixie managed to climb it.

As she got closer and closer to us, I glanced sideways at my sister. I hated her so. Always sniveling, always scared; why did I have to be the one who got us out of trouble? I took my mirror from my other pocket and threw it over my head.

Of course it turned into a glass hill that was slippery enough even the nixie couldn't possibly get on top of it; and that water nixie thought, "Well, I'll just have to go home and get my axe and break this glass hill in two." But by the time she got the blunt axe Ketzia had used to chop at the maple, we had gotten all the way home.

The water nixie had to toddle back to her well.

When we sat down to supper no one noticed my sister and I were covered in muck and smelled. No one knew that we'd disappeared. Neither our mother nor father knew what had happened.

Slowly I realized we wouldn't tell. Ketzia and I never discussed this; it just happened. Yet as soon as I realized this, a hideous rage filled my soul and never departed. I wanted something that never would come—but what?

As I sat by the window box where my mother grew flowers—portulaca, succulents, jade—I came to this understanding.

I glanced over at Ketzia. She was jabbing at a dumpling with her fork and her face expressed hunger. I looked at my mother in her orange and brown apron. She beamed. "They came out nice and soft!" she exclaimed.

"Not soft as mine!" crowed my grandma.

"Mnh, nice and soft," grunted my father. They all were happy eating.

"I hate dumplings," I announced, and was sent to my room without supper. Little did everyone know I could have said something more awful. I could have told about the well, and about what a louse of a young girl I was.

chapter forty-one

"The Louse and the Flea"

A louse and a flea kept house together. They brewed their beer in an eggshell and one day the louse fell in and got scalded. The flea began to scream at the top of her lungs. "Why are you screaming so?" asked the door. "Because Louse has got scalded." At that the door began to creak. A broom in the corner spoke up. "Why are you creaking, Door?" "Haven't I got cause enough to creak?

> Louse has got scalded,
>
> Flea is crying."

At that the broom began to sweep furiously. A cart came along and said: "Why are you sweeping, Broom?" "Haven't I cause enough to sweep?

> Louse has got scalded,
>
> Flea is crying,
>
> Door is creaking."

"In that case I'm going to run," said the cart, and he began to run furiously. He ran past the rubbish heap, and the rubbish heap said: "Why are you running, Cart?" "Haven't I got cause enough to run?

> Louse has got scalded,
>
> Flea is crying,

> Door is creaking,
>
> Broom is sweeping."

"In that case I'm going to burn like mad," said the rubbish heap, and burst into a blaze. A tree, which was growing beside the rubbish heap, said: "Why are you burning, Rubbish Heap?" "Haven't I got cause enough to burn?

> Louse has got scalded,
>
> Flea is crying,
>
> Door is creaking,
>
> Broom is sweeping,
>
> Cart is running."

"In that case I'm going to shake myself," said the tree, and shook himself so hard that all his leaves fell off. A girl who came out with her water pitcher saw him do it and said: "Tree, why are you shaking yourself?" "Haven't I cause enough to shake myself?

> Louse has got scalded,
>
> Flea is crying,
>
> Door is creaking,
>
> Broom is sweeping,
>
> Cart is running,
>
> Rubbish Heap is burning."

"In that case I'm going to smash my water pitcher," said the girl, and smashed her water pitcher. "Girl, why are you smashing your pitcher?" said the spring the water came from. "Haven't I cause enough to smash my pitcher?

> Louse has got scalded,
>
> Flea is crying,
>
> Door is creaking,
>
> Broom is sweeping,

Cart is running,
Rubbish Heap is burning,
Tree is shaking himself."

"Goodness gracious," said the spring. "In that case I'm going to gush." And he began to gush furiously. And they were all drowned in the gushing water, the girl, the tree, the rubbish heap, the cart, the broom, the door, the flea, and the louse, the whole lot of them.

chapter forty-two

M erry could not recall who had first invented the mar-
velous game of The Punish, but she suspected it was
her sister. She knew it had not been her mother, for her
mother had taught them only the most wholesome of games
in their youth: Old Maid, hopscotch, four-square. The Punish was a game with many intricate rules stitched together
from one's mood, truly a wonder.

On one brisk autumn Sunday, after the Golds had returned home from Grandma and Grandpa's house in the
city—having drunk lots of soda and eaten boiled tongue,
deviled eggs, tuna, pizza, chocolate and yellow cake—Merry
and Ketzia were put in the bedroom for their afternoon nap.
Through orange sheer curtains the red maple leaves were
a more fierce and gorgeous beauty than the girls had ever
seen.

The setting was perfect for punishment: a backdrop that
burned.

But Merry felt strangely bored. Wandering in her socks
to the hallway, she heard her footsteps echo downstairs; this
was strange, she thought, for usually only her brother's footsteps resounded like that; but perhaps this was good, for if

anyone would get in trouble for wandering off during nap-time, it would be him who was suspected. She felt blurry in her pajamas so early in the day, but Mrs Gold thought childhood sacred and had them wear flannel pajamas with pictures of horses upon them.

With two small hands, Merry lifted the giant dictionary off its resting place on the hall desk. She lugged it back to the room where Ketzia slept, breathing too loudly, filling the room with her hot little life. Glancing from Ketzia to the woods to the lions with manes, Merry felt sick. It seemed the beauty of autumn was punishing enough.

So Merry dropped the large dictionary on Ketzia's stomach. She hoped it would stop Ketzia's breath from coming out so hard, make it quieter. But all the dictionary did was make Ketzia dream about padding down the hallway in her pink nightgown to pee.

Perched on the edge of her sister's bed, Merry stared out orange curtains to maples lining the street. "How strange and good it looks out there," Merry thought—and then she began to weep and weep. Downstairs watching football, her parents knew nothing of this.

A Riddling Tale

For a long and vexing time when I was younger, my sisters and I were turned into flowers. Shoved into dirt near the sidewalk, we were allowed inside only when the sky became dark. Then, my mother would come and dig out our roots and carry us gingerly into the kitchen. There I always fixed her some coffee—spoonfuls of crystals dropped into hot water.

We were all pink flowers with tiny petals called *portulaca*. Our stems were long and waxen.

One evening while I heated the teapot, I overheard my little sister say, "If you plant me again, I'll go crazy."

When my mother put us back out the next morning the hot sun turned the edges of our petals pale brown. But our little sister had been allowed to stay inside, and so her flower remained very pretty.

That evening, when the dirt cooled beneath us, my other sister and I quietly wept. Like dew, our tears wet our flowers and those that grew beside us. After that, we grew even bigger and bloomed. No one noticed.

Here is the question for you. How did my mother know which of us said she'd go crazy, when we were identical flowers among the wandering Jew in pots in the kitchen? That riddle is easy to answer. The little sister had closed up her flower; ours were open and wet with dew.

Another riddle is harder to answer. Why was I sent from my mother the next year, banished to hell in the city?

chapter forty-four

To Whom Does This Merry Belong?

Once upon a time a businessman and a shoemaker lived in a town. My father, Mr Gold, was the businessman. The shoemaker's shop, a mile from our home, was full of wonderful smells: leather, oil, and rubber.

The shoemaker's son and I went to school together, and as it happened, I was a very poor pupil and the shoemaker's son was the best in the class. We often played together at the park—when we played, I was Queen of the Monkey Bars and he was King of the Sandbox.

He was a good boy—kind and gentle. His nickname was Lamb, while my own was The Mean. It's no wonder our parents tried to keep us apart. They agreed I'd be bad for him.

But as we grew older he began to help me with math. My father the businessman had hopes I would excel in the subject. It seemed that with the help of the shoemaker's son, I could impress my father.

But one day my parents decided to drop by school to see how I was doing. They sneaked through the woods—a path from our house led to the recess yard—and stood by the fence. There they saw that the girls played with the girls and the boys played with the boys, except for me and the shoemaker's son, who sat together beneath a tree.

It was unfortunate, but at the moment they saw me I was throwing my arms around him to thank him for explaining division. I was hugging him very hard in affection; even when young, when I was happy with something I simply wanted to devour it whole!

Alas, there had been troubles already with me and the boys, so my parents were worried and sent me to a different school, in a different, newer, nearby town. No one knew me there.

However, after school I would still go to the town center to visit Peter—that was the shoemaker's son. And oh, that shoemaker's shop was the most pleasing place I ever had been: it seemed everything in it was brown, my favorite color. And it was underground; you got to it from a brick stair. Always I loved things underground, like basements where secrets hung from the walls, clammy and damp. Or like a well.

It was cool down in the shoemaker's shop and it was dark and no one spoke; in order even to speak to the shoemaker, you took a number!

But soon my father went to drop off some shoes, and saw me down there. I'll admit it: we were kissing beside the shoelaces. He saw us there and grabbed me by the collar and dragged me home. The shoemaker said nothing, nothing at all. I wasn't a very suitable girl—not like my sister, whom everyone called Clever Ketzia. I was Mean Merry. My parents forbade me to see Peter again.

There were things I did with other boys after that because I was angry.

Still, I visited Peter at his father's shop. I sneaked out in the middle of night to do it and as I walked down the streets of the suburb I heard everyone sleeping, making those loud breathing noises of humans. People slept with their windows open so their breathing noises wafted into the night willy-nilly—it was awful, the sounds of so many humans asleep in their rooms. I shut my ears to the breathing and listened instead to the night.

I could hear the stars talking, it seemed. They told me in cold voices that no one loved me, and that I was capable of nothing.

When I saw Peter at the shoemaker, he gave me a ring made of silver. "I don't love you, Merry," he said, "but put this ring on and remember to do your best." I slipped the ring onto my finger and felt suddenly ill. I ran from him and ran and ran, and when I got home I drank a whole bottle of something I found in the garage. It was named after a pirate.

I barely breathed that night; my human noises were too weak to blow from the windows at all. And in the morning, I showed no sign of life. This was the first of many such experiences, and not the last to land me in the hospital.

I suppose Peter never wanted to see me again after that. And who can blame him? He was just a childhood friend, nothing more.

Still, when I was deep in my slumber from drinking that stuff, I dreamed that Peter and I lived together above a dressmaker's shop. In the shop we sold frocks of beautiful fabric that I myself had sewn; and Peter, having learned his own father's trade, made boots and slippers to go with them. The dresses were made of silk and organza. The shoes of worn, rugged leather. All had been hand-stitched by us. Sewn up tight and perfect.

In the dream, my father saw me behind the counter and said "But you look just like my daughter!" He started to weep. Then he left the shop and wandered around town, completely forlorn.

Peter led me by the hand to the small courtyard behind the shop, bounded by an iron fence. There, he was growing a withering vine.

"To whom does this vine belong?" I asked him. It was lovely—with red flowers on it and hummingbirds feeding from them.

He strung the vine gently around my throat like a shoe-lace or like a noose. The vine belonged to me.

This was my dream. When I woke up in the hospital, either very soon after this dream or maybe later, I knew only to feed on the nectar, whether vodka or gin, absinthe or rum, whiskey or beer or champagne.

Whenever I'd come home—during school breaks or from the hospital, or finally on days off from work—I would skulk around my parents' house until my mother asked me "Don't you have anything to do besides watch me vacuum?" She'd sort of shove the vacuum up against my feet where I sat, to dislodge me.

Then I'd go to the shoemaker's shop. There I'd hang my-self with a shoelace, and Peter would find and cut me down. I'd sit outside on the brick staircase lined with metal fencing. I'd kick my feet and remember things. People would walk past me with their deli, dry cleaning, books from the library, and bags of broken down shoes. Finally, I'd walk back to my parents' dead-end street and hope they'd invite me to dinner.

Do you know that there are strange creatures living behind my house that need only shade and sun and dirt? Pink lady's slippers, Indian pipes, puffers, and bleeding hearts.

Often I go into the woods, sit near a toadstool, and marvel at their fortune.

THE END

ILLUSTRATION CREDITS

Page 29   "Dach Weh!" from *Struwwelpeter: oder lustige Geschichten und drollige Bilder fur Kinder von 3-6 Jahren* (Frankfurt am Main: Literarische anstalt von Rutten & Loning, 1900)

Page 39   "Topsy Turvy" © Karin Stack

Page 59   "Sewing" © Wayne Eardley

Page 85   "Sing Every One," Illustration from *Hansel and Gretel* (1812), illustrated by Walter Crane, 1886

Page 97   "The Mice"/NGC 4676 (ACS Full Field Image). Courtesy of NASA

Page 107   "Sewing Labels," courtesy of Merry Gold

Page 129   Illustration from "The Little Mermaid" by Arthur Rackham. Courtesy of the Estate of Arthur Rackham/The Bridgeman Art Library

Page 135   "Marigold," J.J. Granville, *The Flowers Personified (Les Fleurs Animée)*, 1855

Page 157   "Black Cat," courtesy of Merry Gold

For their unflagging efforts on behalf of this novel and so many other books, I gratefully acknowledge Ralph Berry, Brenda Mills, and Tara Reeser at FC2, and the staff of the University of Alabama Press. I would also like to thank my colleagues and students in the Department of English at the University of Alabama, the graduate students in the Form and Theory of Fairy Tales seminar at the University of Massachusetts, Maria Tatar, Jack Zipes, and Donald Haase, for their creative and intellectual support. Finally, I must thank Lydia, Kieran, Donna, Willy, and Brent…for everything.